Mrs. 'Arris Goes to New York

Books by Paul Gallico

Mrs. 'Arris Goes to New York

by

Paul Gallico

Drawings by Mircea Vasiliu

Doubleday & Company, Inc., Garden City, New York, 1960

To Ginnie

The Marquis Hypolite de Chassagne is of course not
the Ambassador of France to the United States. He
is only the benevolent genie of a latter day fairy tale.
Nor will you find Mrs. Harris, Mrs. Butterfield, or
the Schreibers at the addresses given, for everyone
and everything in this story is fictitious. If, however,
the characters herein do not resemble someone you
have encountered somewhere, sometime, then the
author has failed to hold up a small mirror to life
and extends his regrets to one and all. P.W.G.

ISBN-13: 978-0-7394-8040-3

One   Mrs. Ada Harris and Mrs. Violet Butterfield, of numbers 5 and 7 Willis Gardens, Battersea, London, respectively, were having their nightly cup of tea in Mrs. Harris's neat and flower-decorated little flat in the basement of No. 5.

Mrs. Harris was a charwoman of that sturdy London breed that fares forth daily to tidy up the largest city in the world, and her lifelong friend and bosom companion, Mrs. Butterfield, was a part-time cook and char as well. Both looked after a fashionable clientele in Belgravia, where they met varying adventures during the day, picking up stray and interesting pieces of gossip from the odd bods for whom they worked. At night they visited one another for a final cup of tea to exchange these tidbits.

Mrs. Harris was sixtyish, small and wiry, with cheeks like frosted apples, and naughty little eyes. Mrs. Harris, who had a very efficient and practical side, was inclined to be romantic, an optimist, and see life in rather simplified divisions of either black or white. Mrs. Butterfield, likewise sixtyish, was stout, billowy, a kindly, timorous woman, the complete pessimist, who visualized everyone, including herself, as living constantly on the brink of imminent disaster.

Both of these good ladies were widows of long standing. Mrs. Butterfield had two married sons, neither of whom contributed to her support, which did not surprise her. It would have astonished her if they had. Mrs. Harris had a married daughter who lived in Nottingham and wrote to her every Thursday night. The two women lived useful, busy, and interesting lives, supported one another physically and spiritually, and comforted one another in their loneliness. It had been Mrs. Butterfield who by taking over Mrs. Harris's clients   5 temporarily had enabled Mrs. Harris a year or so ago to make a flying trip to Paris for the exciting and romantic purpose of buying a Dior dress, which same trophy now hung in Mrs. Harris's wardrobe as a daily reminder of how wonderful and adventurous life can be to one who has a little energy, stick-to-itiveness, and imagination to make it so.

Snug and cozy in Mrs. Harris's neat flat, by the glow of lamplight, the teapot hot and fragrant beneath the yellow-flowered tea cozy Mrs. Butterfield had knitted Mrs. Harris for Christmas, the two women sat and exchanged the events of the day.

The radio was turned on, and from it issued a series of dismal sounds attributed to a recording made by one Kentucky Claiborne, an American hillbilly singer.

"So I sez to the countess, 'It's either a new 'Oover or me,' " recounted Mrs. Harris. "Stingy old frump. 'Dear Mrs. 'Arris,' sez she, 'cawn't we make it do another year?' Make do indeed! Everytime I touch the flippin' thing I get a shock clear down to me toes. I gave 'er a ultimation. 'If there ain't a new 'Oover on the premises tomorrow morning, the keys go through the door,' " Mrs. Harris concluded. Keys to a flat dropped through the mail slot was the charwoman's classic notice of resignation from a job.

Mrs. Butterfield sipped at her tea. "There won't be one," she said gloomily. "I know that kind. They'll put every penny on their own back, and that's all they care."

From within the speaker of the little table radio Kentucky Claiborne moaned.

"Kiss me good-by, ol' Cayuse.
Kiss me, ol' hoss, don' refuse.

Bad men have shot me—
Ah'm afeered they have got me,
Kiss me good-by, ol' Cayuse."

"Ugh!" said Mrs. Harris. "I can't stand any more of that caterwauling. Turn it off, will you, love?"

Mrs. Butterfield obediently leaned over and switched off the radio, remarking, "It's real sad, 'im being shot and wanting 'is 'orse to kiss 'im. Now we'll never know if it did."

This, however, was not the case, for the people next door apparently were devotees of the American balladier, and the saga of tragedy and love in the Far West came seeping through the walls. Still another sound penetrated the kitchen in which the two women were sitting, a dim thud and then a wail of pain, which was followed immediately by the turning up of the wireless next door so that the twang of the guitar and Kentucky Claiborne's nasal groaning drowned out the cries.

The two women stiffened immediately, and their faces became grim and deeply concerned.

"The devils," whispered Mrs. Harris. "They're 'avin' a go at little 'Enry again."

"Ow, the poor lamb," said Mrs. Butterfield. And then, "I can't 'ear 'im any more."

"They've turned up the wireless so we carn't." Mrs. Harris went to a place in the wall between the houses where evidently at one time there had been a connecting hatchway and the partition was thinner, and pounded on it with her knuckles. An equal measure of pounding came back almost instantly from the other side.

8   Mrs. Harris put her mouth close to the partition and

shouted, "'Ere, you stop hitting that child. Do you want me to call the police?"

The return message from the other side of the partition was clear and succinct. A man's voice. "Aw, go soak yer 'ead. 'Oo's 'itting anyone?"

The two women stood close to the wall, listening anxiously, but no more sounds of distress came through, and soon the stridency of the wireless likewise diminished.

"The devils!" hissed Mrs. Harris again. "The trouble is they don't hit 'im 'ard enough so it shows, or we could call the N.S.P.C.C. I'll give them a piece of me mind in the morning."

Mrs. Butterfield said sorrowfully, "It won't do no good, they'll only take it out on 'im. Yesterday I gave 'im a piece of cake left over from me tea. Cor', them Gusset brats was all over 'im, snatching it away from 'im before he ever got a mouthful."

Two tears of frustration and rage suddenly appeared in Mrs. Harris's blue eyes, and she delivered herself of a string of very naughty and unprintable words describing the Gusset family next door.

Mrs. Butterfield patted her friend's shoulder and said, "There, there, dear, don't excite yourself so. It's a shyme, but what can we do?"

"Something!" Mrs. Harris replied fiercely. Then repeated, "Something. I can't stand it. 'E's such a dear little tyke." A gleam came into her eyes. "I'll bet if I went to America I'd soon enough find his dad. 'E's got to be somewhere, hasn't 'e? Eating his 'eart out for 'is little one, no doubt."

A look of horror came into Mrs. Butterfield's stout face, 9

her duplicate chins began to quiver and her lips to tremble. "Ada," she quavered, "you ain't thinkin' of goin' to America, are you?" Fresh in her memory was the fact that Mrs. Harris once had made up her mind that the one thing she wanted more than anything else in the world was a Dior dress, and that she had thereupon scrimped and saved for two years, flown by herself to Paris, and returned triumphantly with the garment.

To Mrs. Butterfield's great relief there apparently *were* limits to her friend's potentialities, for Mrs. Harris wailed, " 'Ow can I? But it's breaking me 'eart. I can't stand to see a child abused. 'E ain't got enough meat on 'is bones to sit down on."

All of Willis Gardens knew the story of little 'Enry Brown and the Gussets, a tragedy of the aftermath of the war and, alas, too often repeated.

In 1950, George Brown, a young American airman stationed at an American air base somewhere, had married a waitress from the nearby town, one Pansy Cott, and had by her a son named Henry.

When at the close of his tour of enlistment George Brown was posted for return to the United States, the woman refused to accompany him, remaining in England with the child and demanding support. Brown returned to the United States, mailing back the equivalent of two pounds a week for the care of the infant. He also divorced his wife.

Pansy and Henry moved to London, where Pansy got a job, and also met another man who was interested in marrying her. However, he wanted no part of the child, and the price of his making her an honest woman was that she get rid of it. Pansy promptly farmed out little Henry, then aged three, with a family by the name of Gusset (who lived in Willis Gardens and had six children of their own), married her lover, and moved to another town.

For three years the pound a week which Pansy had agreed to pay the Gussets for little Henry's keep (thus taking a clear pound of profit for herself) continued to come, and Henry, while not exactly overfed on this bounty, was not much worse off than the members of the Gusset brood. Then one day the pound did not arrive, and never again turned up thereafter. Pansy and her new husband had vanished and could not be traced. The Gussets had an address for the father, George Brown, somewhere in Alabama. A letter sent thither demanding funds was returned stamped "Unknown at this address." The Gussets realized they were stuck with the child, and after that things were not so good for Henry.

From then on it became evident to the neighborhood that the Gussets, who anyway had a kind of Jukes-family reputation, were taking it out on the child. Little 'Enry had become a matter of deep concern to the two widows who lived beside the Gussets, but in particular to Mrs. Harris, who found that the unhappy little orphan-by-law touched her heart, and his plight invaded her dreams of the day and of the nighttime.

If the Gussets had been more brutally cruel to little Henry, Mrs. Harris could have done something immediate and drastic in co-operation with the police. But Mr. and Mrs. Gusset were too smart for that. No one knew exactly what it was Mr. Gusset did to eke out a living for his family, but it took place in Soho, sometimes during the night, and the general opinion held that it was something shady.

Whatever it was, it was known that the Gussets were particularly anxious to avoid the attentions of the police, and therefore, as far as little Henry was concerned, remained strictly within the law. They were well aware that the police were not able to take action with reference to a child except in cases of extreme and visible cruelty. No one could say exactly that the boy was starving or suffering from injuries. But Mrs. Harris knew his life was made a constant hell of short rations, cuffs, slaps, pinches, curses, as the Gussets revenged themselves upon him for the stoppage of the funds.

He was the drudge and the butt of the slatternly family, and any of their two girls and four boys ranging from the ages of three to twelve could tweak, kick, and abuse him with impunity. But worst of all was the fact of the child growing up without love or affection of any kind. On the contrary, he was hated, and this both Mrs. Harris and Mrs. Butterfield found the most painful of all.

Mrs. Harris had had her share of hard knocks herself; in her world these were expected and accepted, but she had a warm and embracing nature, had successfully brought up a child of her own, and what she saw of the little boy next door and the treatment meted out to him began to assume the nature of a constant pain and worry, and something which was never too far or entirely out of her thoughts. Often when she was, as dictated by her nature, blithe, gay, lighthearted and irrepressible about her work, her clients, and her friends, there would come the sudden sobering thought of the plight of little 'Enry. Then Mrs. Harris would indulge in one of her daydreams, the kind that a year or so ago had sent her off to the great adventure of her life in Paris.

The new daydream took on the quality of the romantic fiction of which Mrs. Harris was a great devotee via magazines many of her clients sloughed off upon her when they were finished with them.

In Mrs. Harris's opinion, and transferred to the dream, Pansy Cott, or whatever her new name now happened to be, was the villainess of the story, the missing airman Brown the hero, and little 'Enry the victim. For one thing, Mrs. Harris was convinced that the father was continuing the support of his child and that Pansy was simply pocketing the money. It was all Pansy's doing—Pansy who had refused to accompany her husband to America, as was her wifely duty; Pansy who had withheld the child from him; Pansy who, in order to satisfy a lover, had farmed out the little boy to this beastly family; and finally, Pansy who had vanished with the loot, leaving the boy to his awful fate.

George Brown, on the other hand, was one of nature's noblemen; in the intervening years in all likelihood he would have made his fortune, as Americans did. Perhaps he had remarried, perhaps not, but whatever and wherever, he would be pining for his lost 'Enry.

This estimate of George Brown was based upon her experience with American GIs in England, whom she had invariably found friendly, warmhearted, generous, and particularly loving and kind to children. She remembered how during the war they had unfailingly shared their rations of sweets with the children surrounding their bases. They were inclined to be loud, noisy, boastful, and spendthrift, but when one got to know them, underneath they were the salt of the earth.

They were, of course, the richest people in the world, and

Mrs. Harris reared a kind of fantasy palace where George Brown would now be living, and where little 'Enry too could be enjoying his birthright if only his dad knew of his plight. She had no doubt but that if somehow Mr. Brown could be found and advised of the situation, he would appear upon the scene, wafted on the wings of a faster-than-sound jet, to claim his child and remove him from the tyranny and thralldom of the nasty Gussets. It wanted only a fairy godmother to give the knobs of Fate a twist and set the machinery going in the right direction. It was not long before, so affected was she by the plight of little 'Enry, Mrs. Harris began to see herself as that fairy godmother.

Somehow in the dream she was transplanted to the great United States of America, where by a combination of shrewdness and luck she turned up the missing George Brown almost at once. As she narrated the story of little 'Enry to him tears began to flow from his eyes, and when she had finished he was weeping unashamedly. "My good woman," he said, "all of my riches can never repay you for what you have done for me. Come, let us go at once to the airplane and set out to fetch my little boy home where he belongs." It was a very satisfactory dream.

But as has been noted before, Mrs. Harris was not wholly given to spinning webs of fantasy. She was hardheaded, practical, and realistic about the situation of little Henry, the Gussets, and the knowledge that no one had been able to locate the father, coupled with the fact that no one had really attempted to do so. Underneath the dreams was a growing conviction that if only given an opportunity she could manage to find him, a conviction not at all diminished by the fact that all she knew of him was that his name had been George Brown, and he had been in the American Air Force.

Two   Deep in her heart, Mrs. Harris was well aware that for her a trip to America was as remote as a trip to the moon. True, she had managed to cross the English Channel, and the airplane had made the Atlantic Ocean just another body of water over which to zoom, but the practical considerations of expense and living, etc., put such a journey well out of reach. Mrs. Harris had achieved her Paris visit and heart's desire through two years of scrimping and saving, but this had been a kind of lifetime effort. It had taken a good deal out of her. She was older now and aware that she was no longer capable of making the effort to amass the necessary number of pounds to finance such an expedition.

True, *l'affaire* Dior had been sparked by the winning of a hundred pounds in a football pool, without which Mrs. Harris might never have undertaken the task of amassing another three hundred and fifty. She continued to play the pools, but without the blazing conviction which sometimes leads the face of fortune to smile. She also knew very well that that kind of lightning never struck twice in the same place.

Yet, at the very moment that little Henry, under the cover of the abysmal gargling of Kentucky Claiborne, was being cuffed about in the kitchen of No. 3 Willis Gardens, and sent to bed yet another night insufficiently nourished, Fate was   15 already laying the groundwork for an incredible change in the life not only of himself, but likewise Ada Harris and Mrs. Butterfield.

There was no miracle involved, nothing more supernatural than two sets of men facing one another on either side of the directors' table in the board and conference room of a gigantic Hollywood film and television studio six thousand miles away, glaring at one another with all the venom that can be mustered by greedy men engaged in a battle for power.

Seven hours, one hundred and three cups of coffee, and forty-two Havana Perfectos later, the malevolence of the glares had not diminished, but the battle was over. A cablegram was dispatched which had consequences both direct and indirect in the lives of a strange assortment of people, some of whom had never even heard of North American Pictures and Television Company, Inc.

Amongst the clients for whom Mrs. Harris "did" not only with regularity but enthusiasm, since she had her favorites, were Mr. and Mrs. Joel Schreiber, who had a six-room flat on the top floor of one of the reconditioned houses in Eaton Square. Joel and Henrietta Schreiber were a middle-aged, childless American couple who had made their home in London for the last three years, where Mr. Schreiber had acted as European representative and distribution manager for North American Pictures and Television Company.

It was through the kindness of Henrietta Schreiber originally that Mrs. Harris had been able to change her hard-earned pounds for the necessarily exportable dollars which had enabled her to pay for her Dior dress in Paris. Neither of them had had any inkling that they were breaking the law in doing this. As Mrs. Schreiber saw it, the pound notes were remaining with them in England, and not leaving the country, which was what the British wanted, wasn't it? But then Mrs. Schreiber was one of those muddled people who never quite catch on to the way things operate, or are supposed to operate.

With the daily help and advice of Mrs. Harris she had been able to accustom herself to keeping house in London, shopping in Elizabeth Street and doing her own cooking, while Mrs. Harris's energetic appearance for two hours a day kept her flat immaculate. Any sudden changes or problems turning up were likely to send Mrs. Schreiber into a flutter. As one who before coming to England had been compelled to cope with the type of servants available in Hollywood and New York, Henrietta was a fervent admirer of Mrs. Harris's speed, efficiency, skill at making the dust fly, and above all her ability to cope with almost any situation which arose.

Joel Schreiber, like Napoleon's everyman soldier who carried a marshal's baton in his knapsack, possessed an imaginary president's corporation seal in his brief case. A hardheaded businessman who had worked his way up in North American Pictures from office boy to his present position, but always on the business side, he also had nourished dreams of arts and letters, and what he would do if he were president of North American, a contingency so remote that he never even so much as discussed it with his Henrietta. The kind of job Mr. Schreiber had did not lead to presidencies, formations of policy, and conferences with the great and near-great stars of the film and television world.

Yet when the already-mentioned conference in Hollywood   17

was over and the cablegram dispatched, it was to none other than Joel Schreiber, with instructions to move his offices as well as his domicile to New York for the tenure of a five-year contract as president of North American Pictures and Television Company, Inc. Two power combines battling for control of North American, neither strong enough to win, and facing exhaustion, had finally agreed upon Schreiber, a dark-horse outsider, as a compromise candidate and eventual president of North American.

Following upon the cablegram which reached Schreiber at his office that afternoon were long-distance telephone calls, miraculous "conference" conversations spanning oceans and continents, in which five people—one in London, two in California, two in New York—sat at separate telephones and talked as though they were all in one room, and by the time Mr. Schreiber, a stocky little man with clever eyes, returned home that early evening, he was simply bursting with excitement and news.

There was no holding it in, he spilled it all in one load upon the threshold as he entered his flat. "Henrietta, I'm IT! I got news for you. Only it's real news. I'm president of North American Pictures, in charge of everything! They're moving the offices to New York. We've got to leave in two weeks. We're going to live there in a big apartment on Park Avenue. The company found one for me already. It's a double penthouse. I'm the big squeeze now, Henrietta. What do you think of it?"

They were a loving and affectionate couple, and so they
18 hugged one another first, and then Mr. Schreiber danced

Henrietta around the apartment a little, until she was breathless and her comfortable, matronly figure was heaving.

She said, "You deserve it, Joel. They should have done it long ago." Then, to calm herself and collect her thoughts, she went to the window and looked out onto the quiet, leafy shade of Eaton Square, with its traffic artery running down the middle, and with a pang thought how used she had become to this placid way of life, how much she had loved it, and how she dreaded being plunged back into the hurly-burly and maniac tempo of New York.

Schreiber was pacing up and down the flat with excitement, unable to sit down, as dozens of new thoughts, thrills, and ideas connected with his newly exalted position shot through his round head, and once he stopped and said, "If we'd had a kid, Henrietta, wouldn't he have been proud of his old man at this minute?"

The sentence went straight to Henrietta's heart, where it struck and quivered like a dart thrown into a board. She knew that it was not meant as a reproach to her, since her husband was not that kind of man—it had welled simply from the need he had felt so long to be a father as well as a husband. And now that overnight he had become Somebody, she understood how the need had become intensified. When she turned away from the window there were tears brimming from the corners of her eyes and she could only say, "Oh, Joel, *I'm* so proud of you."

He saw at once that he had hurt her, and, going to her, he put his arm around her shoulder and said, "There, Henrietta, I didn't mean it like it sounded. You don't need to cry. 19

We're a very lucky couple. We're important now. Think of the wonderful times we're going to have in New York, and the dinner parties you're going to give for all them famous people. You're really going to be the 'hostess with the mostes',' like in the song."

"Oh, Joel," Henrietta cried, "it's been so long since we've lived in America, or New York—I'm frightened."

"Pshaw," comforted Mr. Schreiber. "What you got to be frightened of? It'll be a breeze for you. You'll do wonderful. We're rich now, and you can have all the servants you want."

But that was just what Mrs. Schreiber *was* worrying about, and which continued to worry her the following morning long after Mr. Schreiber had floated away to his office on a pink cloud.

Her confused and excited imagination ranged over the whole monstrous gamut of international slatterns, bums, laggards, and good-for-nothings who sold their services as "trained help." Through her harassed mind marched the parade of Slovak, Lithuanian, Bosnian-Herzegovinian butlers or male servants with dirty fingernails, yellow, cigarette-stained fingers, who had worked for her at one time or another, trailing the ashes of their interminable cigarettes all over the rugs behind them. She had dealt with oxlike Swedes, equally bovine Finns, impudent Prussians, lazy Irish, lazier Italians, and inscrutable orientals.

Fed up with foreigners, she had engaged American help, both colored and white, live-in servants who drank her liquor and used her perfume, or daily women who came in the morning and departed at night usually with some article of her clothing or lingerie hidden upon their persons. They didn't know how to dust, polish, sweep, rinse out a glass, or clean a piece of silver; they left pedestal marks on the floor where, immobile like statues, they had leaned for hours on their brooms, doing nothing. None of them had any pride of house or beautiful things. They smashed her good dishes, china, lamps and bric-a-brac, ruined her slip covers and linens, burned cigarette holes in her carpets, and wrecked her property and peace of mind.

To this appalling crew she now added a long line of sour-faced cooks, each of whom had made her contribution to the gray hairs that were beginning to appear in her head. Some had been able to cook, others not. All of them had been unpleasant women with foul dispositions and unholy characters, embittered tyrants who had taken over and terrorized her home for whatever the length of their stay. Most of them had been only a little batty; some of them just one step from the loony bin. None of them had ever shown any sympathy or kindliness, or so much as a single thought beyond the rules they laid down for their own comfort and satisfaction.

A key rattled in the door, it swung open, and in marched Mrs. Harris carrying her usual Rexine bag full of goodness-only-knows what that she always brought with her on her rounds, and wearing a too-long, last year's coat that someone had given her, with a truly ancient flowerpot hat, relic of a long-dead client, but which now by the rotation of styles had suddenly become fashionable again.

"Good morning, ma'am," she said cheerily. "I'm a bit early this morning, but since you said you was 'aving some friends for dinner tonight, I thought I'd do a real good tidying up and 'ave the plyce lookin' like apple pie."

21

To Mrs. Schreiber, her mind hardly cleared of the ghastly parade of remembered domestic slobs, Ada Harris looked like an angel, and before she knew what she was doing she ran to the little char, threw her arms about her neck, hugged her, and cried, "Oh, Mrs. Harris, you don't know how glad I am to see you—how very glad!"

And then unaccountably she began to cry. Perhaps it was the comfort of the return hug and pat that Mrs. Harris gave her, or release from the emotional strain following the good news of her husband's promotion, but she sobbed, "Oh, Mrs. Harris, something wonderful has happened to my husband. We're going to New York to live, but I'm so frightened—I'm so terribly afraid."

Mrs. Harris did not know what it was all about, but there was no doubt in her mind as to the cure: she put down her carryall, patted Mrs. Schreiber on the arm, and said, "There, there now, dear, don't you take on so. Just you let Ada 'Arris make you a cup of tea, and then you'll feel better."

It was a comfort to Mrs. Schreiber to let her do so, and she said, "If you'll make yourself one too," and as the two women sat in the kitchen of the flat sipping their brew, Mrs. Schreiber poured it all forth to her sympathetic sister-under-the-skin, Mrs. Harris—the great good fortune that had befallen her husband and herself, the change that would take place in their lives, the monstrous, gaping, two-storied penthouse apartment that awaited them in America, the departure in two weeks, and above all, her qualms with the servant problem. With renewed gusto she narrated for Mrs. Harris's appreciative ears all of the domestic horrors and catastrophes that awaited her on the other side of the Atlantic. It relieved her to do so, and gave Mrs. Harris a fine and satisfying sense of British superiority, so that she felt an even greater affection for Mrs. Schreiber.

At the conclusion of her narrative she looked over at the little apple-cheeked char with a new warmth and tenderness in her own eyes and said, "Oh, if only there were someone like you in New York to help me out, even if just for a little until I could get settled."

There then fell a silence, during which time Henrietta Schreiber looked across the table at Ada Harris, and Ada Harris over the empty teacups regarded Henrietta Schreiber. Neither said anything. It would not have been possible by any scientific precision instrument known to man to have measured any appreciable interval as to which of them was hit by the great idea first. If such a thing were possible, the two pennies dropped at one and the same moment. But neither said anything.

Mrs. Harris arose, clearing the tea things, and said, "Well, I'd best be gettin' on with me work, 'adn't I?" and Mrs. Schreiber said, "I suppose I ought to look over the things I mean to take with me." They both then turned to what they had to do. Usually when they were in the flat together they nattered, or rather Mrs. Harris did and Mrs. Schreiber listened, but this time the little char worked in thoughtful silence, and so did Mrs. Schreiber.

That night when Mrs. Harris foregathered with Mrs. Butterfield, she said, "'Old onto your hair, Vi, I've got something to tell you. We're going to America!"

Mrs. Butterfield's scream of alarm rang through the area   23 with such violence that doors and windows were opened to check its source. After Mrs. Harris had fanned her back to coherence, she cried, "'Ave you gone out of yer mind? Did you say *we're* going?"

Mrs. Harris nodded complacently. "I told yer to 'ang onto yer hair," she said. "Mrs. Schreiber's going to ask me to go along with her until she can get settled into 'er new plyce in New York. I'm going to tell 'er I will, but not unless she tykes you along as cook. Together we're going to find little 'Enry's father!"

That night when Mr. Schreiber came home Henrietta broke a long period of taciturnity on her part by saying, "Joel, don't be angry with me, but I have an absolutely hopelessly mad idea."

In his present state of euphoria nothing was likely to anger Mr. Schreiber. He said, "Yes, dear, what is it?"

"I'm going to ask Mrs. Harris to come to New York with us."

Schreiber was not angry, but he was certainly startled. He said, "What?"

"Only for a few months perhaps, until we get settled in and I can find someone. You don't know how wonderful she is, and how she keeps this place. She knows how I like things. Oh, Joel, I'd feel so—secure."

"But would she come?"

"I don't know," Henrietta replied, "but—but I think so. If I offered her a lot of money she'd have to come, wouldn't she? And I think she might just because she likes me, if I begged her."

24

Mr. Schreiber looked doubtful for a moment and said, "A Cockney char in a Park Avenue penthouse?" But then he softened and said, "If it'll make you feel better, baby, go ahead. Anything you want now, I want you should have."

Three   Exactly fourteen and one-half hours after Mrs. Harris had told Mrs. Butterfield she was about to be propositioned by Mrs. Schreiber to go to America, it happened. Mrs. Schreiber proposed the very next morning, shortly after Mrs. Harris had arrived, and was enthusiastically accepted upon one condition—namely, that Mrs. Butterfield be included in the party, and at a wage equal to that promised to Mrs. Harris.

"She's me oldest friend," explained Mrs. Harris. "I've never been away from London more than a week at a time in me life. If I 'ad 'er with me, I wouldn't feel so lonely. Besides, she's a ruddy good cook—cooked for some of the best 'ouses before she retired from steady work. You ask old Sir Alfred Welby who he got 'is gout from."

Mrs. Schreiber was almost beside herself with joy at the prospect of not only having Mrs. Harris to look after her during the first months of her return to the United States, but also at one and the same time acquiring a good cook who would get on well with the little char and keep her from getting too lonely. She knew Mrs. Butterfield and liked her, for she had subbed for Mrs. Harris during the latter's expedition to Paris to acquire her Dior dress. "But do you think she would come?" she asked of Mrs. Harris anxiously.   25

"At the drop of a brick," replied the latter. "Adventurous, that's what she is. Always wantin' to rush off into the unknown. Sometimes I can 'ardly keep 'er back. Oh, she'll come all right. Just you leave it to me to put it to 'er in the right way."

Mrs. Schreiber was delighted to do so, and they began to discuss details of departure—Mr. Schreiber was planning to sail in the French liner SS *Ville de Paris* from Southampton within ten days—as though everything was all set and arranged for the two of them.

Mrs. Harris chose the psychological moment to move the attack upon her friend, namely, the witching hour of that final mellow cup of tea they shared before retiring, and this time in Mrs. Butterfield's ample kitchen, well stocked with cakes and biscuits, jams and jellies, for as her figure indicated, Mrs. Butterfield liked to eat well.

At first it seemed as though Mrs. Harris had committed a tactical error in approaching her friend on her own home grounds instead of getting her away from her familiar surroundings, for Mrs. Butterfield was adamant in her refusal to budge and appeared to have an answer to every argument put forth by Mrs. Harris.

"What?" she cried. "Me go to America at my age, where they do all that inflation and shooting and young people killing one another with knives? Don't you read the papers? And let me tell you something else, if you go it'll be the death of you, Ada 'Arris—don't say I didn't warn you."

Mrs. Harris tried the financial offensive. "But, Violet, look at the money she's offered to pay you—American wages, a hundred quid a month and keep. You don't earn that much in three months 'ere. You could rent your flat while you was away, yer widow's pension'd be piling up, you'd have no expenses of any kind—why, you'd like as not have five hundred quid by the time you came 'ome. Look what a 'oliday you could 'ave with that. Or put it into Premium Bonds and win a thousand quid more. You'd never 'ave to do another stroke of work."

"Money ain't everything," Mrs. Butterfield countered. "You'd know that, Ada 'Arris, if you read your Bible more. The root of all evil, that's what it is. Who's got the most trouble in this world, who's always being dragged into court and getting their nymes in the papers? Millionaires. I can make enough for me needs right 'ere, and that's where I'm stayin'. Anyway, I wouldn't go to that Soda and Gomorrow, what they say New York is, for five hundred quid a month."

Mrs. Harris moved up her intercontinental missile with megaton warhead. "What about little 'Enry?" she said.

Mrs. Butterfield regarded her friend with some alarm. "What about 'im?" she asked, to gain time, for in the excitement and terror of Mrs. Harris's proposition she had quite forgotten who and what lay behind it all.

"To find 'is dad and give the poor little tyke a decent life, that's what's all about 'im, Violet Butterfield, and I'm surprised and ashymed at you forgettin'. If you've 'eard it once, you've 'eard me say a 'undred times, if I could only get to America I'd find 'is dad and tell 'im where 'is kid was and what was 'appening to 'im. Well now, 'ere's our chance to go and do just that, and you ask me what about little 'Enry! Don't you love 'im?"

This was almost attacking below the belt, and Mrs. Butterfield let out a howl of protest. "Ow, Ada, 'ow can you say such a thing? You know I do. Ain't I always feedin' 'im up and cuddling 'im like a mother?"

"But don't you want to see 'im 'appy and safe with his father?"

"Of course I do," said Mrs. Butterfield, and then produced to her own great surprise out of her own locker an atomic-ray defense, which nullified Mrs. Harris's attack. "'Oo's to look after 'im while you're away if I go too? What's the use of you turning up 'is old man only to 'ave 'im come over 'ere and find the poor little tyke starved to death? One of us 'as got to stay 'ere."

There was intrinsically so much logic in this statement that for the moment Mrs. Harris was nonplussed and could not think of an answer, and so with an extraordinary heaviness about her heart she looked down into her teacup and said simply, "I do wish you'd come to America with me, Vi."

It was now Mrs. Butterfield's turn to look at her friend with astonishment. Sincerity brought forth an equal measure of sincerity in herself. Gone now were all the subterfuges, and she replied, "I don't want to go to America—I'm afraid to go."

"So am I," said Mrs. Harris.

Mrs. Butterfield's astonishment turned now to amazement. "What!" she cried. "You, Ada 'Arris, afraid! Why, I've known you for more than thirty-five years, and you've never been afraid of anything in your life."

"I am now," said Mrs. Harris. "It's a big step. It's a strange country. It's a long way off. Who's to look after me if anything happens? I wish you were coming with me. One never knows, does one?"

It might have sounded like irony, this sudden switch in the accustomed roles of the two women: Mrs. Harris the adventurous optimist suddenly turned into a kind of Butterfield timorous pessimist. But the truth was that there was no irony whatsoever in her remark. It was just that the realization had suddenly come upon her of the enormity of the undertaking into which she had thrust herself so lightheartedly and with her usual sense of excitement and adventure. New York was not only a long way off, it would be totally different from anything she had ever experienced. True, Paris had been utterly foreign, but if you looked at a map, Paris was just across the street. America would be English-speaking, it was true, and yet in another sense more foreign than France, or perhaps even China. She was going to uproot herself from that wonderfully secure and comfortably fitting London which had sheltered her for all her life and about whose streets and rhythm and noises and manifold moods she knew her way blindfolded. And she was no longer young. She knew of the many British wives who, having married Americans, had come running home, unable to adjust themselves to American life. She was sixty-one, a sixty-one that felt full of energy and brimming with life, it is true, but one never did know, did one? Supposing she fell ill? Who in a strange land would provide the necessary link between herself and her beloved London? Yes, for that instant she was truly and genuinely afraid, and it showed in her eyes. Violet Butterfield saw it there.

29

"Oh dear," said the fat woman, and her round chins began to quiver. "Do you mean it, Ada? Do you really need me?"

Mrs. Harris eyed her friend, and knew that she really did want this big, bulky, helpless but comfortable woman to lean on a little. "Yes, love," said Mrs. Harris, "I do."

"Then I'll come with you," said Mrs. Butterfield, and began to bawl. Mrs. Harris started to cry too, and immediately the two women were locked in one another's arms, weeping together for the next few minutes, and having a most lovely time.

The die, however, had been cast, and the trip was on.

Anyone who knew the worth of Mrs. Harris and Mrs. Butterfield to their clients would not have been surprised, had they come into Belgravia, to have found large sections of this exclusive area decorated with black crepe hung out after the two widows had notified their clients that within one week's time they were departing for the United States and would not be available for at least three months thereafter, and perhaps longer.

However, such is the toughness of the human spirit, as well as the frame, and likewise so stunning the news and excitement engendered by the fact that Mrs. Harris and Mrs. Butterfield were going out to what some of them still persisted in referring to as "the colonies," that the blow was taken more or less in stride.

Had the two women merely announced a one- or two-day or a week's hiatus, there would then have been such revolutions in the area as to shake every mews, crescent, square, and lane—but three months meant forever, and constituted one of the hazards of modern living. With a sigh most of them resigned themselves to renewed visits to the employment office, and a further period of trial and error until another such gem as Mrs. Harris or Mrs. Butterfield could be found.

𝓕𝓸𝓾𝓻 Ever afterward Mrs. Harris swore that the thought of kidnaping little Henry from the disgusting Gussets, stowing him away aboard the *Ville de Paris,* and taking him bodily to his father in America would never have occurred to her but for the astonishing coincidence of the episode in the home of the Countess Wyszcinska, whose London *pied-à-terre* in Belgrave Street Mrs. Harris brightened between the hours of five and six. It was that same countess with whom she had had the contretemps over the new Hoover and who, contrary to the gloomy prognostications of Mrs. Butterfield, had known what was good for her and produced one.

Thus, she was in the flat of the countess when a parcel arrived for that august lady from her eighteen-year-old nephew in Milwaukee, Wisconsin. The contents of the parcel proved to be the most awful eyesore the countess had ever beheld—a horribly encrusted beer stein with an imitation silver lid and "Souvenir of Milwaukee" emblazoned on its side. Unfortunately, so thoroughly had this revolting *objet d'art* been wrapped in and stuffed out with old newspapers that it had arrived in unbroken condition.

The countess, with an expression of distaste about her aristocratic countenance, said, "Ugh! What in God's name?" 31

And then, aware of Mrs. Harris's interested presence, quickly corrected herself and said, "Isn't it lovely? But I just don't know where to put it. There's so much in this little place already. Would you like to take it home with you, Mrs. Harris?"

Mrs. Harris said, "Wouldn't I just. 'Souvenir of Milwaukee' —I might be going there to visit when I'm in America."

"Well, just get it out of here——I mean, I'm glad you like it. And throw all that trash away while you're at it," pointing to the papers that had preserved its life. Thereupon the countess departed, wondering what had got into chars nowadays that they seemed always to be traveling.

Left to herself, Mrs. Harris then indulged in one of her favorite pastimes, which was the reading of old newspapers. One of her greatest pleasures when she went to the fishmonger's was to read two-year-old pages of the *Mirror* lying on the counter and used for wrapping.

Now she picked up a page of a newspaper called the Milwaukee *Sentinel*, eyed the headline DOMINIE SEDUCED SCHOOLGIRL IN HAYLOFT, enjoyed the story connected therewith, and after that leafed through the other pages of the same instrument of public service until she came to one of young brides, young grooms-to-be, and young married couples.

Always interested in weddings, Mrs. Harris gave these announcements more undivided attention, until she came upon one which caused her little eyes almost to pop out of her head, and led her to emit a shriek. "Ruddy gor'blimey— it's 'im! It's 'appened! I felt it in me bones that something would."

What she was looking at was the photograph of a handsome bridal couple over which was the caption, "Brown-Tracey

Nuptials," and underneath the story under the dateline of Sheboygan, Wisconsin, January 23: "The wedding was celebrated here today at the First Methodist Church on Maple Street, of Miss Georgina Tracey, daughter of Mr. and Mrs. Frank Tracey of 1327 Highland Avenue, to Mr. George Brown, only son of Mr. and Mrs. Henry Brown of 892 Delaware Road, Madison, Wisconsin. It was the bride's first marriage, the groom's second.

"The bride, one of the most popular graduates of Eastlake High School, has been a leader in the social activities of the younger debutante set. The groom, aged 34, an electronics engineer, was formerly in the U. S. Air Force, stationed in England. The couple will make their home in Kenosha, Wisconsin."

Clutching the paper fiercely between her thin, veined hands, Mrs. Harris performed a little solo dance about the countess's drawing room, shouting, "It's 'im! It's 'im! I've found little 'Enry's father!" There was not the least shadow of doubt in her mind. He was handsome; he resembled little 'Enry in that he had two eyes, a nose, a mouth, and ears; he was of the right age; he was well-to-do, had a noble look about his eyes, as Mrs. Harris had imagined him, and now was married to a fine-looking girl, who would be just the mother for little 'Enry. Popular, the paper said she was, but Mrs. Harris also noted that she had a good, open countenance, and nice eyes. What clinched it and made it certs was the name of Mr. Brown's father—Henry Brown: of course the grandchild would be named after him.

Mrs. Harris ceased her dance, looked down upon the precious photograph, and said, "George Brown, you're going   33 to get your baby back," and at that moment, for the first time, the thought of abstracting little 'Enry from the Gussets and of taking him to his father immediately smote her between the eyes. True, she didn't have his address, but there would be no difficulty in locating him once she got herself and little 'Enry to Kenosha, Wisconsin. If this was not a sign from On High as to where her duty lay and what she ought to do about it, Mrs. Harris did not know signs from Above, which she had been encountering and interpreting more or less successfully ever since she could remember.

Little Henry Brown was aged eight in terms of the tenure of his frail body, eighty in the light of the experience of the harsh and unhappy world into which that body had been ushered. In his brief sojourn he had learned all of the tricks of the persecuted—to lie, to evade, to steal, to hide—in short, to survive. Thrown on his own in the concrete desert of the endless pavements of London, he very early acquired the quickness of mind and the cunning needed to outwit the wicked.

Withal, he yet managed to retain a childish charm and innate goodness. He would never scupper a pal or do the dirty on someone who had been kind to him. Someone, for instance, like the two widow charladies, Mrs. Ada Harris and Mrs. Violet Butterfield, in whose kitchen he was now momentarily concealed, involved in a thrilling and breathless conspiracy.

He sat there looking rather like a small gnome, gorging himself on tea and buns to the point of distention—since one of the things life had taught him was whenever he came across any food that appeared to be unattached, the thing to do was to eat it quickly, and as much of it as he could hold —while Mrs. Harris unfolded the details of the plot.

One of Henry's assets was his taciturnity. Among other things he had learned to keep his mouth shut. He was eloquent rather by means of a pair of huge, dark, sad eyes, eyes filled with knowledge that no little boy of that age should have, and which missed nothing that went on about him.

Because he was thin and somewhat stunted in growth, his head had the appearance of being too large and old, rather an adult head, with a shock of darkish hair, underneath which was a pale and usually dirty face. It was to his eternal credit that there was still some youth and sweetness left in him— adversity had not made him either mean or vengeful.

Whatever the steps he took to make life as easy for himself as possible under the circumstances, they were dictated purely by necessity. He rarely spoke, but when he did it was to the point.

And now as Mrs. Harris continued to unfold yet more details of the most fascinating scheme ever devised to free a small boy from hideous tyranny and guarantee him three square meals a day, he sat silently, his mouth stuffed full of bun, but nodding, his huge eyes filled with intelligence and understanding while Mrs. Harris enumerated each point of what he was to do when, where, and under various circumstances. In these same eyes was contained also considerable worship of her.

It was true, he loved the occasional cuddle pillowed upon the pneumatic bosom of Mrs. Butterfield, though he did not go for too much of that soft stuff, or would not let himself, 35 but it was he and Mrs. Harris who were kindred souls. They recognized something in one another, the independent spirit, the adventurous heart, the unquenchable soul, the ability to stand up to whatever had to be stood up to, and get on.

Mrs. Harris was not one to fuss and gush over him, but she addressed him like an equal, for equal they were in that nether world of hard and unremitting toil to feed and clothe oneself, where life is all struggle and the helping hands are one's own.

In so many ways they were alike. For instance, no one had ever heard Henry complain. Whatever happened to him, that's how things were. No one had ever heard Mrs. Harris complain either. Widowed at the age of thirty, she had raised, educated, and married off her daughter, and kept herself and her self-respect, and all on her hands and knees with a scrubbing brush, or bent over mop and duster, or sinks full of dirty dishes. She would have been the last person to have considered herself heroic, but the strain of simple heroism was in her, and Henry had it too. He also had that quick understanding that gets at the heart of the situation. Whereas Mrs. Harris had to go into long and elaborate explanations of things to Mrs. Butterfield, and she did so with great patience, little Henry usually got it in one, and would nod his acquiescence before Mrs. Harris was halfway through exposing what she had on her mind.

Now when Mrs. Harris had finished rehearsing step by step how the plan was to work, Mrs. Butterfield, who for the first time was hearing what seemed to her to be the concoction of a madwoman, threw her apron over her head and began to rock and moan.

" 'Ere, 'ere, love, what's wrong?" said Mrs. Harris. "Are you ill?"

"Ill!" cried Mrs. Butterfield. "I should think so! Whatever it's called, what you're doing, it's a jyle offense. You can't get away with it. It'll never work."

Little Henry stuffed the last of a sugar bun into his mouth, washed it down with a swig of tea, wiped his lips with the back of his hand, and, turning his large eyes upon the quivering figure of Mrs. Butterfield, said simply, "Garn, why not?"

Mrs. Harris threw back her head and roared with laughter. "Oh, 'Enry," she said, "you're a man after me own 'eart."

Five   Like all great ideas and schemes born out of Genius by Necessity, Mrs. Harris's plan to smuggle little Henry aboard the SS *Ville de Paris* at Southampton had the virtue of simplicity, and one to which the routine of boarding the ship with its attendant chaos, as Mr. Schreiber had carefully explained to her, lent itself beautifully.

Since the Schreibers were going first-class and the two women tourist, they would not be able to travel together, and he had rehearsed for her the details of exactly what they would have to do—the departure by boat train from Waterloo, the arrival at the pier at Southampton where, after passing through Customs and Immigration, they would board the tender for the trip down the Solent, and thus eventually would enter the side of the liner and be shown to their cabin, and thereafter the French line would take over.

To these instructions Mrs. Harris added a vivid memory of an instance when she had been at Waterloo to take a suburban train and at one of the gates had witnessed what appeared to be a small-sized riot, with people milling and crowding, children shrieking, etc., and, inquiring into the nature of this disturbance, had been informed that it was merely the departure of the boat train at the height of the season.

As Mrs. Harris's scheme was outlined to her, even that perpetual prophetess of doom, Mrs. Butterfield, outdid herself with tremblings, groans, cries, quiverings, claspings of hands together, and callings upon heaven to witness that the only possible result could be that they would all spend the rest of their natural lives in a dungeon, and she, Mrs. Violet Butterfield, would have no part of it. She had agreed to embark upon this harebrained voyage across an ocean waiting to engulf them, to a land where death lurked at every corner, but not to make disaster doubly sure by beginning the trip with a kidnaping and a stowing-away.

Mrs. Harris, who, once she had what she considered a feasible idea in her head, was not to be turned from it, said, "Now, now, Violet—don't take on so. A stitch in time will help us to cross over those bridges." And then with remarkable patience and perseverance managed to overcome practically all of her friend's objections.

Her intrinsic plan was based upon recollections of childhood visits to Clacton-on-Sea with her Mum and Dad, and the outings they used to enjoy on the excursion steamers to Margate, a luxury they occasionally permitted themselves. Poor and thrifty, her folks could manage the price of two

38

tickets, but not three. When it came time to pass through the gates and encounter the ticket taker, little Ada had been taught to detach herself from her parents and, seeking out a large family with five or more youngsters, join up with them until safely through the gates. Experience had taught them that in the Sunday crush the harassed ticket taker would not be able to distinguish whether it was five or six children who had passed him, and the equally harassed father of the family would not notice that he had suddenly acquired an extra little girl. Once they were inside, by the time paterfamilias, perhaps aware that something was a little unusual about his brood, instituted a nose count, little Ada would have detached herself from this group and joined up with her parents again.

Moreover, there was a reserve gambit in case a large enough family failed to turn up. Father and mother would pass through on their tickets, and a few seconds later little Ada would let forth a wail. "I'm lost! I'm lost! I've lost my Mummie!" By the time this performance had reached its climax and she was restored to her frantic parents, nobody thought of collecting a ticket from her. The excursion proceeded happily.

Mrs. Butterfield, who in her youth had had similar experiences, was forced to concede that neither of these devices had ever failed. She was further put off her prophetic stroke by Mrs. Harris's superior knowledge as a world traveler.

"Don't forget, dearie," said Mrs. Harris, "it's a *French* boat. Muddle, that's their middle name. They can't get nothing done without carrying on shouting and waving their arms. You'll see."

Mrs. Butterfield made one more attempt. "But once 'e's in 39 our room, won't they find 'im?" she quavered, her chins shaking.

Mrs. Harris, now slightly impatient, snorted, "Lor', love, use yer loaf. We've got a barfroom, 'aven't we?"

This was indeed true. So thrilled had Mrs. Schreiber been with her luck in acquiring two servants whom she liked and trusted, that she had persuaded her husband to procure for them one of the better rooms available in tourist class on the liner, one of a few with a bathroom connected, and intended for larger families. Mrs. Harris had been shown the accommodations on a kind of skeleton plan of the ship, and while she did not exactly know what part the barfroom would play once aboard the lugger, it loomed large in her mind at least as a retreat in which parties could momentarily retire during alarm or crisis.

Six   As may be imagined, the departure of Mrs. Harris and Mrs. Butterfield for the United States was an event that shook the little street in Battersea known as Willis Gardens to its Roman foundations, and all of their friends and neighbors, including the unspeakable Gussets, turned out to bid them Godspeed. Such was the excitement engendered by the arrival of the taxicab at No. 5, and the piling of ancient trunks and valises on the roof and next to the driver's seat, that no one thought about or noticed the absence of little Henry Brown.

40   Like all persons unused to traveling, the two women had

taken far more with them than they would ever need, including photographs, ornaments and little knickknacks from their homes which meant something to them, and thus the inside of the cab was similarly stuffed with luggage, leaving, it seemed, barely room for the stout figure of Mrs. Butterfield and the spare one of Mrs. Harris to squeeze in.

Appraised that they were actually off to America, the cab driver was deeply impressed, and became most helpful and solicitous, and treated the two ladies with the deference one accords to royalty, lifting and fastening their boxes and suitcases, and playing to the crowd gathered for the farewell with a fine sense of the dramatic.

Mrs. Harris accepted all of the deference done her and the interest and excitement of friends and neighbors with graciousness, mingling affectionate farewells with sharp directions to the cab driver to be careful of this or that piece of baggage; but poor Mrs. Butterfield was able to do little more than palpitate, perspire, and fan herself, since she could not rid her mind of the enormity of what they were about to perpetrate, or cease to worry about the immediate future, beginning within the next few minutes, and whether it would come off.

The attitude of the Gussets was one of grudging interest, coupled with impudence, which bespoke their feeling of good riddance. Among other things, the departure of the two women meant to them an undisturbed period of abuse of the child who had been entrusted to their care.

It had actually to a great extent been Mrs. Harris who had kept their cruelty within bounds, for they were a little afraid of her and knew that she would not hesitate to involve them   41 with the police if there was a case. Now, with pairs of eyes and ears removed from their bailiwick, they could let themselves go. The Gusset children were going to have a field day, and Mr. Gusset, when things had gone wrong with one of his shady deals in Soho and little Henry happened to fall afoul of him, was not going to have to restrain himself. The child was in for a sticky time of it, and delight at the departure of his two protectresses was written all over the faces of the Gussets—mother, father, and offspring.

Finally the last valise had been stowed and secured, the taxi driver had taken his seat behind the wheel and animated the engine, perspiring Mrs. Butterfield and sparkling Mrs. Harris took their places in the space left for them in the interior of the cab, each clutching a small nosegay of flowers tied with a bit of silver ribbon thrust into their hands at the last moment by friends, and they drove off to a cheer and individual cries of "Good luck!"—"Tyke care of yerselves" —"Send us a post card"—"Don't fergit to come back"— "Give me regards to Broadway"—"Don't fergit to write," and "May the Good Lord look after you."

The cab gathered momentum, Mrs. Butterfield and Mrs. Harris turning and looking out through the rear window to see their friends waving and cheering still and gazing after them, with several of the Gusset children cocking a snook in their direction.

"Ow, Ada," quavered Mrs. Butterfield, "I'm so frightened. We oughtn't to be doing it. What if ——?"

But Mrs. Harris, who herself had been considerably nervous during the departure and had been playing something of a role, now indeed took command of the expedition and pulled herself together. "Be quiet, Vi!" she commanded. "Nuffink's going to happen. Blimey, dearie, if I didn't think you were going to give the show away. Now don't fergit when we get there—you keep your eye peeled out the back." Therewith she tapped upon the window behind the driver with a penny, and when that individual cocked a large red ear in the direction of the opening she said, "Go round the corner through Gifford Plyce to 'Ansbury Street—there's a greengrocer there on the corner . . . his nyme is Warbles."

The cab driver chose a bad moment to joke. "I thought you lydies said you was going to Hamerica," and was surprised at the asperity of the reply he received from Mrs. Harris.

"Do as you're told and you won't gather no flies," she said, for she too was nervous approaching that moment when dreams which seem so easy of realization are turned into action which very often is not.

The taxi drew up in front of the shop, where Mr. Warbles was on the pavement tearing some tops off carrots for a customer.

Mrs. Harris said, " 'E would 'ave to be outside," and added a naughty word. Just then the greengrocer was hailed from within and answered the call.

"Now!" Mrs. Harris said fiercely to Mrs. Butterfield, who was already peering anxiously out of the back window. "Do you see anyone?"

"I don't know," quavered Mrs. Butterfield. "I don't fink so. Leastways, nobody we know."

Mrs. Harris leaned forward to the opening in the window and whispered into the large red ear, " 'Onk yer 'orn three times."

Mystified and intimidated, the driver did so. From behind some stacked-up crates of cabbages the figure of a small, dark-haired boy came charging, looking neither right nor left, straight for the door of the cab which Mrs. Harris now held open. With the combined speed and agility of a ferret, the boy wriggled his way beneath the luggage piled inside the cab and vanished.

The door slammed shut. "Waterloo," hissed Mrs. Harris into the ear.

"Well, I'm blowed," said the taxi driver to himself at this curious performance, and put his machine into gear. That the two respectable charladies who were just departing for America from a respectable neighborhood might be engaging in a casual bit of kidnaping never entered his head.

Seven It is a fact that nothing is quite as noticeable as a child that wants to be noticed, but the converse is likewise true, that there is nothing equally self-effacing as a child desiring to be vanished, and who in particular is permitted to operate in a crowd.

This was a technique known both to Mrs. Harris and little Henry, and thus when the Schreibers were seen descending upon them along the bustling station platform at Waterloo, causing Mrs. Butterfield to utter a little yelp of terror, it was no problem at all for Mrs. Harris to vanish Henry. She gave him a slight pat on his bottom, which was the prearranged signal, at which he simply moved off from them and stood   45 next to somebody else. Since the Schreibers had never seen him before, they now did not see him at all, except as somebody else's child, standing by a piece of luggage and gazing heavenward, apparently singing hymns to himself.

"Ah, there you are," said Mrs. Schreiber breathlessly. "Is everything all right? I'm sure it will be. Have you ever seen so many people? I did give you your tickets, didn't I? Oh dear! It's all so confusing."

Mrs. Harris tried to soothe her mistress. "Now, there, dearie," she said, "don't you fret. Everything's right as rain. We'll be fine. I've got Violet here to look after me." The sarcasm was lost on Mrs. Butterfield, who only perspired more profusely and fanned herself more freely. It seemed to her that the Schreibers *must* ask, "Who's that little boy with you?" even though at the moment he wasn't.

Mr. Schreiber said, "They're perfectly all right, Henrietta. You forget that Mrs. Harris went to Paris and back all by herself, and stayed a week."

"Of course," Mrs. Schreiber fluttered, "I'm afraid you won't be allowed to visit us on the ship." She blushed suddenly at the implication of the class distinction, both un-American and undemocratic, and then added quickly, "You know how they are about letting anyone go from one part of the ship into the other. I mean—if there's anything you need, of course, you can send us a message . . . Oh dear . . ."

Mr. Schreiber got his wife out of her embarrassment by saying, "Sure, sure. They'll be all right. Come on, Henrietta, we'd better get back to our seats."

Mrs. Harris gave them the thumbs up as they departed. And as the Schreibers retreated, almost imperceptibly little

Henry moved over and was with them again. "That was fine, love," applauded Mrs. Harris. "You're a sharp one. You'll do."

All the while she was speaking her bright, buttony, wicked little eyes were taking in the people surrounding them, travelers as well as friends coming to see them off, and easily separated by the fact that the travelers looked nervous and worried, and the visitors gay and unencumbered.

Standing in front of an open carriage door several compartments away was a large family of Americans, a father and mother surrounded by an immense pile of hand luggage and an indeterminate number of offspring—that is to say, indeterminate between five and six, due to the fact that they were wriggling, jumping about, escaping, playing hide-and-seek, so that not even Mrs. Harris was able successfully to count them. After observing them for an instant, Mrs. Harris took little Henry by the arm, pointed the group out to him, and, leaning down, whispered into his ear, "Them there."

Little Henry did not reply, but only nodded gravely, and with his sad, wise eyes, studied the antics of the group in order that later he might blend the more perfectly with them.

It would be more suspenseful and dramatic to be able to report that Mrs. Harris's plans were scuppered, or even scrambled by the usual malevolent fates, but the point is they simply were not.

Smoothly, efficiently, and without a hitch, they moved from Waterloo to Southampton, from Southampton to the tender, and from the tender to the great black, porthole-studded wall crowned by cream superstructure and gay red funnel of the SS *Ville de Paris.* Whenever anyone remotely resembling a   47 ticket collector, conductor, Immigration or Customs official appeared in the offing, quietly and inconspicuously little Henry became a temporary member of the family of a Professor Albert R. Wagstaff, teacher of medieval literature at Bonanza College, Bonanza, Wyoming. With her unerring instinct Mrs. Harris had even managed to select an absent-minded professor for the deal.

If Dr. Wagstaff was at times not quite certain whether his family consisted of six or seven members, he was also equally befuddled as to the number of pieces of luggage accompanying him. Each time he counted the articles they added up to a different sum, until his irritated wife shouted, "Oh, for God's sakes, Albert, stop counting! It'll either all be there or it won't."

In his usual state of terror where Mrs. Wagstaff was concerned, Dr. Wagstaff said, "Yes, dear," and immediately stopped counting not only luggage, but children, even though from time to time there did seem to be one extra. Thus little Henry's task was made comparatively simple, and, as said before, there were no hitches.

One moment containing a slight measure of tension occurred when the three of them—Mrs. Harris, Mrs. Butterfield, and little Henry—were safely ensconced in Tourist Cabin No. A134, a roomy enough and rather charmingly decorated enclosure with two lower and upper berths, closet space, and a bathroom opening off, when heavy footsteps were heard pounding down the companionway and there came a sharp and peremptory knock upon the door.

Mrs. Butterfield's florid countenance turned pink, which

was the best she could do in the way of going pale. She gave a little shriek and sat down, perspiring and fanning. "Lor'," she quavered, "it's all up with us!"

"Dry up," ordered Mrs. Harris fiercely, and then whispered to little Henry, "Just you go into that nice barfroom, dearie, and sit down on the seat, and be quiet as a mouse, while we see who's come to disturb two defenseless lydies traveling to America. You can do your duty if you like."

When Henry had vanished into the bathroom in a matter of seconds, Mrs. Harris opened the cabin door to be confronted by a sweating and frayed-looking steward in white coat with the collar unbuttoned. He said, "Excuse me to disturb, I 'ave come to collect your steamship tickets."

With one eye on Mrs. Butterfield, who now had changed color from pink to magenta, and appeared on the verge of apoplexy, Mrs. Harris said, "Of course you 'ave," and, diving into her reticule, produced them. "'Ot, ain't it?" she said pleasantly. "My friend 'ere's in a proper sweat."

"Ah, *oui*," the steward assented, "I make it cooler for you," and switched on the electric fan.

"Lots of people," said Mrs. Harris. This was like pushing a button releasing the steward's neurosis, and he suddenly shouted and waved his arms. "*Oui, oui, oui*—people, people, people. Everywhere people. They make you to be crazy."

"It's the kids that's the worst, ain't it?" said Mrs. Harris.

This appeared to be an even more potent button. "Oh, la, la," shouted the steward, and waved his arms some more. "You 'ave seen? Keeds, keeds, keeds, everywhere keeds. I go crazy with keeds." 49

"Ain't that the truth," said Mrs. Harris. "I never seen so many. You never know where they are or where they ain't. I don't know how you keep track of 'em all."

The steward said, "*C'est vrai*. Sometimes is not possible." Having blown off steam, he recovered himself and said, "Sank you, ladies. You wish for anything, you ring for Antoine. Your stewardess's name is Arline. She look after you," and he went away.

Mrs. Harris opened the bathroom door, looked in, and said, "All done? That's a dear. You can come out now."

Little Henry asked, "Do I duck in there every time there's a knock?"

"No, pet," Mrs. Harris replied, "not any more. From now on it will be all right."

Which indeed it was, since Mrs. Harris had planted her psychological seed at the right time and in the right soil. In the evening an Antoine even more frayed arrived to turn down the beds. There was little Henry with Mrs. Butterfield and Mrs. Harris. The steward looked at the child and said, "'Ullo, 'oo's this?"

Mrs. Harris, now not gentle, friendly, and conversational as she had been before, said, "'Ullo yourself. What do you mean, 'oo's this? This is little 'Enry, me sister's boy. I'm taking 'im to America to 'er. She's got a job as waitress in Texas."

The steward still looked baffled. "But he was not here before, was he?"

Mrs. Harris bristled. "'E wasn't what? 'Ow do you like that? The child's the happle of me eye and never been out of me sight since we left Battersea."

50

The steward wavered. He said, "*Oui, madame*, but——"

"But nothing," snapped Mrs. Harris, attacking with asperity. "It ain't our fault you Frenchies get excited over nothing and lose your 'eads, come in 'ere shouting about people and kids. You said yourself you couldn't remember all the kids. Well, don't you go forgetting little 'Enry 'ere, or we'll 'ave to 'ave a word with one of the officers."

The steward capitulated. It had been an unusually trying sailing. Down the next hall there was an American family which still did not seem to be able to agree on the number of pieces of luggage and the number of children accompanying them. Besides which he had already turned in his tickets to the purser. The women seemed like honest types, and obviously the child was with them and must have come through Immigration. Long years at sea and coping with passengers had taught him the philosophy of leaving well enough alone, and not bringing about investigations.

"*Oui, oui, oui, madame,*" he soothed, "of course I remember heem. 'Ow you call heem—little Henri? You try not to make a mess in the cabin for Antoine, we'll all have very 'appy voyage."

He did the beds and went out. From then on little Henry was a full-fledged passenger of the SS *Ville de Paris*, with all the privileges and perquisites pertaining thereto. Nobody ever questioned his presence.

Back at No. 3 Willis Gardens, Battersea, the sole repercussion from Mrs. Harris's tremendous coup, which saw little 'Enry removed forever from the custody of the Gussets and now afloat on the briny, took place upon the return of Mr. 51

Gusset from another of his slightly shady transactions in Soho. Mrs. Gusset, who was sparing her feet with a session in the rocking chair while the elder Gusset children coped with dinner in the kitchen, lowered the *Evening News* as her better half appeared, and said, " 'Enry's been missing since this morning. I think maybe he's run away."

" 'As 'e?" replied Mr. Gusset. "That's good." Then, snatching the paper from her fingers, he commanded, "Up you get, old lady," ensconced himself in the vacated rocker, and applied himself to the early racing results in the newspaper.

Eight "Oh dear," said Henrietta Schreiber suddenly, "I wonder if I've done the right thing." She was sitting in front of her mirror in her cabin, putting the final touches to her face. Beside her lay an engraved card of invitation which stated that Pierre René Dubois, Captain of the SS *Ville de Paris*, would be honored by the company of Mr. and Mrs. Joel Schreiber for cocktails in his cabin at seven-thirty that evening. The ship's clock was already showing the hour of seven thirty-five.

"What's that?" said her husband, who, properly accoutered in black tie, had been waiting for ten minutes. "Sure, sure. You look fine. I promise you, Momma, you never looked better. But I think we ought to go now. The French ambassador's going to be there, the steward said."

"No, no," said Henrietta, "I don't mean me, I mean about Mrs. Harris."

"What about Mrs. Harris? Is something the matter?"

"No—I'm just wondering if we've done right taking her and Mrs. Butterfield out of their element. They're so very London, you know. People over here understand about chars and their ways, but ——"

"You mean they'll laugh at us because we've got a couple of Cockneys?"

"Oh no," protested Mrs. Schreiber. "Why, nobody would laugh at Mrs. Harris." She made another attempt upon her eyebrows. "It's just I wouldn't want her to be frightened. Who could she talk to? Who could she have for friends? And you know what snobs people are."

Waiting had made Mr. Schreiber a little impatient. "You should have thought of that before," he said. "She can talk to Mrs. Butterfield, can't she?"

The corners of Mrs. Schreiber's mouth turned down. "Don't be cross with me, Joel. I'm so proud you're president now of North American and I wanted to do everything to make things right for you in New York—and she's such a wonderful help. For all I know she may be back there crying her eyes out and frightened to death among a lot of strangers."

Mr. Schreiber went over and gave her an affectionate pat on the shoulders. He said, "Well, it's too late now. But maybe tomorrow I'll take a walk back to tourist and see how she's getting on. How about coming along now, baby? You couldn't look more beautiful if you worked for another hour. You'll be the best-looking woman there."

Henrietta rested her cheek against his hand for a moment and said, "Oh, Joel, you're so good to me. I'm sorry I get into such a muddle."

53

They emerged from their cabin, where their steward waited to guide them. He took them as far as the private stairway leading to the captain's quarters, which they mounted, to be received by another steward who asked their names. And then led them to the door of the huge cabin from which emerged that distinctive babble of sounds that denotes a cocktail party in full swing. Embedded in these sounds—the clink of glasses and the crosscurrents of conversation—was an impossible sentence which smote the ear of Mrs. Schreiber. "Lor' love yer, the marquis and I are old friends from Paris."

It was impossible simply because it could not be so, and Mrs. Schreiber said to herself, "It's because I was *thinking* of Mrs. Harris just before I came up here."

The steward stepped through the doorway and announced, "Mr. and Mrs. Joel Schreiber," which brought forth a drop in the conversation, and the bustle of all the men rising to their feet.

Entering thus late into a cocktail party there is a confusion of sight as well as sound—one sees everyone, and one sees no one. For an appalling moment Mrs. Schreiber seemed to be aware of another impossibility, one even more unthinkable than the auditory one she had just experienced. It was Mrs. Harris ensconced between the captain and a distinguished-looking Frenchman with white hair and mustache—Mrs. Harris wearing a very smart frock.

The captain, a handsome man in dress uniform with gold braid, said, "Ah, Mr. and Mrs. Schreiber. So delighted you could come," and then with practiced hand swung the circle of introductions—names that Mrs. Schreiber only half heard until he came to the last two, and no mistake about those: "—

His Excellency the Marquis Hypolite de Chassagne, the new French ambassador to your country, and Madame Harris."

There was no doubt about it, it was true! Mrs. Harris was there, apple-cheeked, beady-eyed, beaming, yet not at all conspicuous, and looking as quietly well dressed as, if not better than, most of the women in the room. And somehow it was not the presence of Mrs. Harris so much, but the matter of her appearance which bewildered Henrietta more than anything. All that went through her mind was, *"Where have I seen that dress before?"*

Mrs. Harris nodded graciously and then said to the marquis, "That's 'er I been telling you about. Ain't she a dear? If it 'adn't been for 'er, I never could have got the dollars to go to Paris to buy me dress, and now she's tyking me with 'er to America."

The marquis went over to Henrietta Schreiber, took her hand in his, and held it to his lips for a moment. "Madame," he said, "I am enchanted to meet one with a warm heart that is able to recognize a warm heart and goodness in others. You must be a very kind person."

This little speech, which established Mrs. Schreiber socially for the rest of the voyage, also left her breathless, and she was still staggering under the impact of it all. "But—but you *know* our Mrs. Harris?"

"But of course," replied the marquis. "We met at Dior in Paris, and are old friends."

What had happened was that, having learned from his chauffeur of the presence of Mrs. Harris on board in tourist class, he had said to the captain, who was a friend, "Do you know, Pierre, that you have a most remarkable woman on board your ship?"

"You mean the Countess Touraine?" asked the captain, whose business of course it was to study the passenger list. "Yes, she is enormously talented, though, if I might suggest, a trifle ——"

"No, no," said the marquis. "I am referring to a London scrubwoman—a char, as they call them—who all day long is on her knees scrubbing the floors of her clients in Belgravia, or having her hands in dirty dishwater washing up after them —but if you looked into her wardrobe you would find hanging there the most exquisite creation from the house of Christian Dior, a dress to the value of four hundred and fifty pounds, which she purchased for herself."

The captain was truly intrigued. "What is that you say? But that is utterly astounding. You say this person is aboard my ship. But what is she doing? Where could she be going?"

"Goodness only knows," replied the marquis, "what she is after now in America, what has come into her head to possess. I can only tell you that when a woman such as this makes up her mind to something, nothing can stop her." And thereupon he recounted to the captain the story of Mrs. Harris coming to Paris to buy herself a Dior dress, and how no one with whom she had come into contact had quite been the same thereafter.

When the marquis had finished his tale the captain, even more piqued, and his curiosity aroused, had said, "And this woman is aboard and you say is a friend of yours? Well then, 57 we shall have her up for a drink. I should be honored to meet her."

And thus it was that Mrs. Harris had received exactly the same kind of engraved invitation as had gone out to the Schreibers, except that on the card had been written: "A steward will come for you to your cabin and lead you to the captain's quarters."

Before Mrs. Schreiber was separated from her husband he found time to whisper to her, "Looks like you can stop worrying about Mrs. Harris, don't it?"

That composed and self-assured lady was now chattering happily and unconcernedly with the captain. It seemed that during her visit to Paris she had been taken to a little restaurant on the Seine which was also a favorite of the captain's when he was ashore, and they were comparing notes.

Henrietta's next seated neighbor said to her, "Are you enjoying the voyage, Mrs. Schreiber?" and was somewhat astonished to receive the reply, "Oh, goodness gracious me! Why, it's one that I gave her!" He had, of course, no way of knowing that the dress encasing Mrs. Harris was one that Mrs. Schreiber had made her a present of several years ago after it had outlived its usefulness, and that she had just recognized it.

Nine   Everything went smoothly on the voyage, lulling Mrs. Harris into self-congratulation and a false sense of security. Optimist though she was, life had taught her that frequently when things seem to be going too well, trouble lurked just around the corner. But the routine of the great ship was so wonderful, the food, the company, the entertainment so luxurious, that even Mrs. Butterfield had begun to relax in this *ambiance* and concede that death and destruction might not be quite as imminent as she had imagined.

Three days of all the good things to eat he could stuff into himself, plus sunshine and the love and spoiling lavished on him by the two women, had already begun to work a change in little Henry, filling him out and somewhat relieving the pinched, pale look.

The SS *Ville de Paris* plowed steadily without a tremor of motion through flat calm seas, and as Mrs. Harris said to herself, everything was tickety-boo—yet disaster was no more than forty-eight hours away, and when she became aware of it, it loomed up as so appalling that she did not even take Mrs. Butterfield into her confidence, for fear that in an excess of terror her friend might be tempted to leap overboard.

It all came about through a conversation which took place with the coterie of friends with whom Mrs. Harris had surrounded herself, and at which, fortunately, Mrs. Butterfield happened not to be present.

As usually occurred on these voyages, Mrs. Harris soon found herself a member of a tight little British island which formed itself in the middle of the Atlantic Ocean aboard this floating hotel. It consisted of an elderly and elegant chauffeur, two mechanics from a British firm sent to America to study   59 missile assembly, and a couple from Wolverhampton going over to visit their daughter, who had married a GI, and their grandchild. Mrs. Harris and Mrs. Butterfield made up the set. They were all at the same table, and soon had their deck chairs next to one another. Basically they all spoke the same language and liked and understood one another.

If Mrs. Harris was the life of this party—which indeed she was—the chauffeur, Mr. John Bayswater, "*of* Bayswater," as he himself would say, "and no finer district in London," was the unquestioned leader of the coterie, and looked up to by all.

To begin with, he was not only a chauffeur of long experience—thirty-five years—a small, sixtyish, gray-haired man whose clothes were well cut and in impeccable taste, but he was also a Rolls chauffeur. In all of his life he had never sat in or driven a car of any other make, he had not even so much as ever looked under the bonnet of one. They simply did not exist for him. There was only one car manufactured, and that was the Rolls. A bachelor, he had had a succession of these motor cars instead of wives or mistresses, and they took up his entire time and attention.

But if this were not sufficient cachet, he was also now going out to America as the chauffeur of the Marquis Hypolite de Chassagne, newly appointed ambassador for France in the United States.

He was a happy and contented man, was Mr. John Bayswater, for in the hold of the *Ville de Paris* there traveled the newest, the finest, the most modern and most gleaming Rolls-Royce in two tones of sky and smoke blue, body by Hooper, that he had ever driven. To celebrate the crowning of his

60

diplomatic career by his appointment as ambassador to the United States, the marquis, who had been educated in England and had never got over his fondness for British cars, had treated himself to the finest Rolls that his independent wealth could buy.

When it came to the question of a chauffeur, the Rolls people had been able to secure for him the services of John Bayswater, who had once accompanied the British ambassador to the United States on the same kind of job, one of the most respected and trusted of Rolls-trained drivers.

Mr. Bayswater's estimate of a good or bad job was based not on the employer for whom he worked, but the nature, kind, and quality of the Rolls-Royce entrusted to his care. If the marquis's appointment was the cap to his career, so was the new job to Mr. Bayswater, since he had been commissioned by the Rolls-Royce Company to go into their factory and himself select the chassis and engine. That the marquis had likewise turned out to be an all-right chap and an understanding man as an employer was just so much money for jam.

But there was yet another reason why Mr. Bayswater could assume and hold the leadership in his little group, and that was that of all of them he was the only one who had ever been out to America before. In fact he had made the trip twice—once with a '47 Silver Wraith, a sweet job he had loved dearly, and again with a '53 Silver Cloud, of which he was not quite so enamored but which he knew needed him, and all the more in the strange country.

And it was precisely this knowledge of Mr. Bayswater's of the procedural ceremony upon entering the free and demo-   61 cratic United States of America which put the wind up Mrs. Harris and indicated to her the extent of the trap into which she had led little Henry, Mrs. Butterfield, and herself.

The conversation came about as indicated during the absence of Mrs. Butterfield from the deck chairs, and the couple from Wolverhampton, Mr. and Mrs. Tidder, were expounding on the trials they had had to endure at the hands of American officials before a visitor's visa was granted them to set foot in America. Mrs. Harris listened sympathetically, for she had been through the same routine: references, finger-prints, names of sponsors, financial situation, endless forms to be filled in, and seemingly equally endless interrogations.

"Goodness me," said Mrs. Tidder, whose husband was a retired civil servant, "you would have thought we were going over to burgle a piece of the country." Then she sighed, "Oh well, I suppose one mustn't complain. They gave us our visas, and it's all over now."

Mr. Bayswater put down a copy of the Rolls-Royce monthly bulletin he had been studying, but with half an ear cocked to the conversation, and snorted, "Ho-ho, is that what you think? Wait until you come up against the United States Immigration Inspectors—they'll put you through it. I'll never forget the first time I came over. It was after the war. They had me sweating. You ever heard of Ellis Island? It's a kind of a gaol where they can pop you if they don't like the look of your face. Wait 'til you sit down to have a chat with those lads. If there's so much as a bit of a blur on your passport, or a comma misplaced, you're for it."

Mrs. Tidder gave a little cry of dismay. "Oh dear, is that
really so?"

At the pit of Mrs. Harris's stomach a small, cold stone was forming which she tried to ignore. She said to Mrs. Tidder, "Garn, I don't believe it. It's just people talking. It's a free country, ain't it?"

"Not when you're trying to get into it," Mr. Bayswater observed. "Proper Spanish Inquisition, that's what it is. 'Who are you? Where are you from? How much have you got? Who are you with? Where are you going? When? Why? For how long? Have you ever committed a crime? Are you a Communist? If not, then what are you? Why? Haven't you got a home in England—what are you coming over here for?' Then they start in on your papers. Heaven 'elp you if there's anything wrong with them. You can cool your heels behind bars on their ruddy island until someone comes and fetches you out."

The stone at the pit of Mrs. Harris's tum grew a little larger, colder, and harder to ignore. She asked, trying to make her question sound casual, "Are they like that with kids too? The Americans I knew in London were always good to kids."

"Ha!" snorted Mr. Bayswater again, "not these chaps." And then with another of his rare cultural lapses he said, "They eats kids. A baby in arms is like a bomb to them. If they don't see the name and birth certificate and proper papers for them they don't get through. When the time comes they herd you into the main lounge, and there you are. Queue up until you sit at a desk with a chap in uniform like a prison warder on the other side, with eyes that look right through you, and you'd better give the right answers. I saw one family held up for three hours because some clerk on the other side had   63 made a mistake in one kid's papers. That's the kind of thing they *love* to catch you out on. And after that the Customs— they're almost as bad. Phew! I'll tell you."

The stone was now as large as a melon and as cold as a lump of ice. "Excuse me," said Mrs. Harris. "I don't think I'm feeling quite well. I think I'll go down to my cabin for a bit of a lie-down."

And so there it was. For twelve unhappy hours Mrs. Harris kept the ghastly news and problem bottled up inside her, during which time she also managed to increase its scope and embroider its dangers. And Mr. Bayswater's erudite reference to the Spanish Inquisition, which to Mrs. Harris brought up pictures of dungeons, the rack, and torturers with hot pincers, did nothing to alleviate her uneasiness.

Anything British or even French she would have felt herself, as a London char, equipped to cope with, but Mr. Bayswater had revealed an implacability about the United States Immigration Service and the red tape surrounding entry into the country which, while it might have been somewhat exaggerated, nevertheless left her with a feeling of complete helplessness. There would be no hurly-burly such as had obtained on the station platform at Waterloo and the embarkation pier at Southampton, no friendly, easygoing British Immigration officers with sympathy for a harassed family man, no attaching of himself by little Henry to the brood of pleasant and absent-minded Professor Wagstaff, no little tricks, no concealments. The fact was that little Henry, having no papers of any kind whatsoever, was going to be nabbed.

What appalled Mrs. Harris was not so much the picture of Mrs. Butterfield and herself languishing behind bars in that place of the dread name of Ellis Island (abandoned, it is true, since Bayswater's day), which appeared to be something in the nature of a German or Russian concentration camp, but rather the far more harrowing thought of little 'Enry being impounded and shipped back to London to the mercies of the Gusset family, while she and Mrs. Butterfield would not be there to protect or comfort the youngster. She fretted herself into a state of near exhaustion trying to think of some way that little 'Enry might avoid the tight immigration net that Mr. Bayswater had outlined, but could find none. The way Mr. Bayswater had put it, not a mouse could get itself into the United States of America without proper credentials.

For herself she did not care, but it was not only little 'Enry who would be in dire trouble; she had likewise led her good friend, poor, timorous Mrs. Butterfield, into a situation which might well result in her becoming dangerously ill with fright. And then there were likewise the Schreibers. What would Mrs. Schreiber do when she, Ada Harris, was carried off to gaol at just the moment when Mrs. Schreiber needed her the most?

There was no doubt but Ada Harris was for it, and needed help badly. But to whom to turn? Certainly not Mrs. Butterfield, and she did not wish to alarm the Schreibers until it was absolutely necessary. Her mind then turned to the one man of experience that she knew—Mr. Bayswater—who, although he was the kind of bachelor she knew to be unalterably confirmed, had shown himself slightly partial to her and had already treated her to several ports and lemon in the cocktail lounge before dinner.

So that night when dinner was over and they were repairing up to the smoking room for coffee and a cigarette, Mrs. Harris whispered, "Could I 'ave a word with you, Mr. Bayswater? You being such a traveled man, I need your advice."

"Of course, Mrs. Harris," Mr. Bayswater replied courteously. "I should be happy to give you the benefit of my experience. What was it you wished to know?"

"I think we'd better go up on deck, perhaps, where it's quiet and nobody's around," she said.

Mr. Bayswater looked a little startled at this, but detached himself from the group and followed Mrs. Harris topside to the boat deck of the *Ville de Paris*, where in the starlit darkness, with the great ship leaving a phosphorescent trail behind her, they stood by the rail and looked out over the sea.

They were silent for a moment, and then Mrs. Harris said, "Lumme, now that I've got you 'ere, I don't know how to begin."

Really startled, Mr. Bayswater turned to look at the little char and steel himself. He had preserved his bachelorhood from numerous assaults for some forty-odd years, and did not consider surrendering it now. But all he saw on the face of the small, gray-haired woman standing next to him was concern and unhappiness. She said, "I'm in trouble, Mr. Bayswater."

The chauffeur felt a sudden flood of relief, as well as warm, masculine protectiveness. He found that he was even enjoying being there and having her thus appeal to him. It was a most excellent feeling. He said to her, "Supposing you tell me all about it, Mrs. Harris."

"You know the boy," she said. "Little 'Enry, that is?"

Mr. Bayswater nodded and replied, "M-hm, good kid. Keeps his mouth shut."

"Well," Mrs. Harris blurted, "he isn't mine. He's not anybody's!" And then in a torrent the whole story came pouring forth from her—the Gusset family, the kindly Schreibers, the kidnaping and stowing-away of little 'Enry, and the plan to deliver him to his long-lost father.

When she had finished there was a silence. Then, "Blimey," said Mr. Bayswater, lapsing once again, "that's a nasty one, isn't it?"

"You've been to America before," pleaded Mrs. Harris. "Isn't there something we could do to hide him or get 'im through?"

"Not from those blokes," said Mr. Bayswater. "You'll only make it worse if you do. It's ten times as bad if they catch you trying to evade them. Look here, what about the father? Couldn't we telegraph him to come to the pier, then at least he could stand up for the kid and claim him."

Despite her worries Mrs. Harris was not insensible that Mr. Bayswater had used the word "we" instead of "you," thus including himself in her dilemma, and it gave her a sudden feeling of returning courage and warmth. But it receded almost immediately as she wailed, "But I don't know 'is address yet. I just fink I know where he is going to live, but I've got to find him first, don't you see? It's a 'orrible mess."

Now likewise stymied, Mr. Bayswater nodded and agreed, "It is that."

A tear caught by starshine rolled down Mrs. Harris's cheek. "It's all my fault," she said. "I'm a stupid, fool'ardy old woman. I should have known better."

"Don't say that," said Mr. Bayswater. "You were only trying to do your best for the kid." He fell silent for a moment, thinking, and then said, "Look here, Mrs. Harris, I know you said you knew my boss—the marquis. Is it true what I heard, that you were invited by him up to the captain's cabin for a drink?"

Mrs. Harris gave the elegant-looking chauffeur an odd look, and wondered if he was going to go snobby on her. "Certainly," she replied, "and why not? 'E's an old friend of mine from Paris."

"Well then," said Mr. Bayswater, his idea growing within him to bursting point and the dropping of another aitch, "if you know him that well, why don't you ask 'IM?"

" 'Im, the marquis? Why, what good would that do? 'E's a pal of mine. I wouldn't want to get 'im sent off to Ellers Island or whatever it's called."

"But don't you see," said Mr. Bayswater excitedly, "he's just the very one who could do it. He's a diplomat."

Unlike her, for an instant Mrs. Harris was obtuse. She said, "What's that got to do with it?"

"It means he travels on a special passport, but no one ever even looks at it, no questions asked—V.I.P. and red carpet. I'm telling you, last time I came over with the '53 Cloud, the one with the weak number-three cylinder gasket, it was with Sir Gerald Granby, the British ambassador. We didn't half breeze through on the pier. No Immigration or Customs for him. It was 'How do you do, Sir Gerald?' and 'Welcome to the United States, Sir Gerald. Step this way, Sir Gerald,' and 'Never you mind about those bags, Sir Gerald. Is there anything we can do for you, Sir Gerald?' 'Come right through, your car is waiting, Sir Gerald.' That's how it went, smooth as silk when you've got a diplomatic passport and a title. Americans are awfully impressed by titles. Now just you think about my boss. He's not only the ambassador himself, but a genuine French marquis. Coo, they'll never even notice the kid, and if they do they won't ask any questions. You ask him. I'll bet he'd do it for you. He's a proper gent. Afterwards, when he's got the kid through and onto the pier, you can collect him easy as wink and no trouble to anyone. Well, what do you think?"

Mrs. Harris was staring at him now with her mischievous little eyes shining—no longer from tears. "Mr. Bayswater," she cried, "I could kiss you."

For an instant the hardened bachelor's fears returned to the dignified chauffeur, but in the light of Mrs. Harris's relieved and merry countenance they were dispelled and he patted one of her hands on the rail gently and said, "Save the smacker for later, old girl—until we see whether it's going to come off."

Ten   Thus it was for the second time in twenty-four hours that Mrs. Harris found herself narrating the story of little Henry, the missing father, and her escapade, this time into the attentive ear of the Marquis Hypolite de Chassagne,   69

Ambassador and Plenipotentiary Extraordinary from the Republic of France to the United States of America, in the privacy of his first-class suite aboard the liner.

The white-haired old diplomat listened to the tale without comment or interruption, occasionally pulling at the end of his mustache or stroking the feathers of his tufted eyebrows with the back of a finger. It was difficult to tell from his extraordinarily young-looking and lively blue eyes, or his mouth, often hidden behind his hand, whether he was amused or annoyed at her plea that he attach to his entourage one stateless and paperless British-American semi-orphan and smuggle him into an alien country as his first act as France's representative.

When Mrs. Harris had finished with the tale of her misdeeds, concluding with the advice given her by Mr. Bayswater, the marquis reflected for a moment and then said, "It was a kind and gallant thing for you to do—but a little foolhardy, do you not think?"

Mrs. Harris, sitting on the edge of a chair mentally as well as physically, clasped her hands together and said, "Lor' love me, you're telling me! I suppose I ought to 'ave me bottom whacked, but, sir, if you'd heard 'is cries when they hit him, and 'im not getting enough to eat, what would you have done?"

The marquis reflected and sighed. "Ah, madame, you flatter me into responding—the same, I suppose. But we have now all landed ourselves into a pretty pickle." It was astonishing how anyone who even for the shortest time became associated with Mrs. Harris's troubles immediately took to
70 using the pronoun "we" and counting themselves in.

Mrs. Harris said eagerly, "Mr. Bayswater said that diplomats like yourself 'ave special privileges. You'll get a special carpet to walk on and it'll be 'Yes, Your Excellency. Step this way, Your Excellency. What a nice little boy, Your Excellency,' and before you know it there you'll be on the pier with little 'Enry, and no questions asked. Then I'll come and collect the kid, and you'll 'ave 'is gratitude and mine and his father's forever after."

"Bayswater seems to know a great deal," said the marquis.

"Of course 'e does," said Mrs. Harris. "'E's done it before. He said the last time 'e came to America it was with somebody named Sir Gerald Granby, and it was 'Yes, Sir Gerald. Step this way, Sir Gerald. Never mind about the passport, Sir Gerald ——'"

"Yes, yes," agreed the marquis hastily. "I know, I know."

But the point was that he did not know in actual fact as much as he thought he did about what landing arrangements had been made for him. He was quite well aware that there might be some fuss and ceremony upon his arrival, but not to what extent, though he was also certain that no one would demand to see his credentials until officially and formally he presented them at the White House. The members of his entourage, his secretary, chauffeur, valet, etc., would receive equal consideration, and it was highly improbable that anyone would observe or question a small boy who seemed to be with him, particularly if he were well behaved, as Mrs. Harris had asserted, and given to keeping his mouth shut.

"Would yer?" pleaded Mrs. Harris. "Don't you suppose you might? You'd take to little 'Enry once you saw him. 'E's a dear little lad."

71

The marquis made a gesture with his hand and said, "Shhh—hush for a moment. I want to think."

Mrs. Harris immediately buttoned up her lip and sat with her hands folded, on the edge of the gilt chair, her feet barely touching the ground, and eying the marquis anxiously out of her little eyes that now had lost their impudence and cunning, and were only anxious and pleading.

That august individual did exactly what he said he was going to do—he sat and thought, but he also felt.

It was a curious thing about Mrs. Harris, that she had the power to make people feel the things that she was feeling. In Paris she had let him into the experience of her passion for flowers and beautiful things such as a Dior dress, and the excitement of loving and desiring them. Now here in her simple way she had made him feel her love for a lost child, and the distress that is experienced all too little at the thought of a child suffering. There were millions of children hungry and suffering and abused throughout the world, and heaven forgive one, one never thought about them, and here *he* was thinking about a little starveling being cuffed on the side of the head by an individual named Gusset, whom he had never seen and never would see. How did all this concern him? Looking at Mrs. Harris sitting opposite him on the anxious seat, seeing the frosted-apple cheeks, withered hair, and hands gnarled by toil, he felt that it concerned him very much.

In her own way, during her brief visit to Paris this London char had brought him some happy moments, and even, if one wanted to stretch a point, his ambassadorship might be laid partly at her feet, for she had been instrumental in causing
72 him to aid the husband of a friend she had made in Paris,

Monsieur Colbert, into an important post in the Quai d'Orsay, where within a year he had proved to be a sensational success. Credit for his discovery redounded to the marquis, and might well have played a role in his selection for the coveted and honored post as ambassador to the United States. But even more, she had recalled to him the days of his youth, when he had been a student at Oxford and another charlady, one of her breed, had been kind to him in his loneliness.

The marquis thought to himself, *"What a good woman is Mrs. Harris, and how fortunate I am to know her."* And he thought again, *"What an astonishingly pleasant thing it is to have the power to help someone. How young it makes one feel!"* And here his thoughts permitted themselves to digress to the change that had come over him since his promotion to this post. Prior to that he had been an old man, resigned to saying farewell to the world and engaged in re-examining and enjoying its beauties for the last time. Now he felt full of energy and bustle and had no thought of quitting this life.

And he had a final and highly satisfactory thought on the subject of what it means to be so old and dignified—namely, that people were a little afraid of you. It meant, he thought with an inward chuckle, and reverting to his British education, that you could do as you jolly well pleased in almost any situation, and no one would really dare to say anything. Thus he came to the final thought: What was the harm in helping this good person, and what in fact could go wrong with the simplicity of the scheme? He said to Mrs. Harris, "Very well, I will do as you ask."

This time Mrs. Harris did not indulge in any pyrotechnics of effusiveness of gratitude, but instead, as her naughty sense

73

of humor returned to her, she grinned at him impishly and said, "I knew you would. It ought to be a lark, what? I'll wash his 'ands and face good, and tell him exactly what 'e's got to to. You can rely on him—'e's sharp as a new pin. 'E don't say much, but when he does it's right to the point."

The marquis had to smile too. "Ah, you did, did you?" he said. "Well, we shall see what kind of trouble I land myself in with this sentimental bit of foolishness." Then he said, "We are due to dock at ten o'clock in the morning; at nine o'clock there will be some kind of a deputation coming on board to greet me no doubt at Quarantine—the French consul perhaps—and it would probably be best if the boy were here at that time so that the others became used to seeing him about. I will make arrangements to have you both conducted through to me from tourist class at half past seven in the morning. I will advise my secretary and valet to be discreet."

Mrs. Harris got up and moved to the door. "You're a love," she said, and gave him the thumbs up sign.

The marquis returned it and said, "You are too. It ought to be quite a lark, what?"

Eleven Someone should have warned the marquis about the American press, which was aware that the marquis was the first new ambassador appointed to the United States since de Gaulle came into power; someone likewise should have advised him of and prepared him for the landing arrangements that had been set up for his arrival. The former, however, was completely forgotten, and the latter, through one of those

State Department muddles—surely-so-and-so-will-have-noti-fied-the-ambassador—totally neglected. Everyone thought the other fellow had done it, and nobody had.

The marquis himself, a man of innate modesty, had never considered his own person of importance, and while he anti-cipated an official welcome and a facilitating of entry, he ex-pected no more than that, and upon arriving in the morning meant to have Bayswater drive him to Washington as soon as his car was disembarked.

Thus he was wholly unprepared for the jostling horde of ship newsmen, feature writers, reporters, newspaper photog-raphers, newsreel cameramen, radio and television inter-viewers, technical men, and operators of batteries of portable television equipment who came streaming on board from a grimy tug that drew alongside in Quarantine, and came stamping down the companionways and pelting into his suite to demand his presence for an interview in the press-conference room on the sun deck.

An equal surprise was the trim white government cutter which also leeched itself to the side of the *Ville de Paris*, dis-gorging the official greeter of the City of New York and his henchmen, all wearing red, white, and blue rosettes in their buttonholes, the leaders of both political parties of that same city, along with the deputy mayor, the French consuls of both New York and Washington, members of the permanent staff of the French legation, a half a dozen officials from the State Department, headed by an undersecretary of proper rank and protocol to receive an ambassador, plus a member of the White House staff sent by President Eisenhower as a personal emissary to welcome him. 75

Most of these somehow managed to crowd into the suite, while a band on the cutter rendered the "*Marseillaise*," and before little Henry could flee into the "barroom" where he had been warned by Mrs. Harris to retire should anything untoward happen before the actual going ashore should take place.

He had been scrubbed and polished for the occasion, thrust into a clean shirt and shorts, and, sitting on the edge of a chair with his feet likewise encased in new socks and shoes, he looked like quite a nice little boy, and one not out of place in his surroundings.

Before either the marquis or little Henry knew what was what, or how it happened, they found themselves swept out of the cabin, up the grand staircase, and into the press-conference room crowded to suffocation with inquisitors and facing an absolutely appalling battery of microphones, camera lenses—still, animated, and television—and barrages of questions flung at them like confetti.

"What about the Russians?" "Do you think there'll be a war?" "What is your opinion of American women?" "How about de Gaulle?" "What are you going to do about NATO?" "Do you wear the bottoms of your pajamas when you sleep?" "Do the French want another loan?" "How old are you?" "Did you ever meet Khrushchev?" "Is your wife with you?" "What about the war in Algeria?" "What did you get the Legion of Honor for?" "What do you think about the hydrogen bomb?" "Is it true that Frenchmen are better lovers than Americans?" "Is France going to resign from the Monetary Fund?" "Do you know Maurice Chevalier?" "Is it true that the

Communists are gaining ground in France?" "What do you think of *Gigi?*"

And amongst those questions shouted by male and female reporters and feature writers yet another: "Who's the kid?"

Now it sometimes happens when a press conference is as unruly as this one was, chiefly because most of the press corps had had to get up very early in the morning to go down the bay in a choppy sea to meet the ship, and many of them had hang-overs, that in a barrage of shouted questions, none of which can be heard or answered, one of them will take place in a momentary lull, and thus stick out, and, anxious to get *some* question answered, the reporters will temporarily abandon their own and pick up that particular one.

Thus it became: "Who's the kid? Who's the kid?" "That's right—who's the kid, Your Excellency?" "Who's the boy, Mr. Ambassador?" And then everybody quieted down to await the answer.

Seated together behind the conference table at the head of the room, the venerable statesman turned and looked down at the strange small boy with the somewhat too-large head and plaintive face, half as though he expected the explanation to come from him.

The small boy likewise turned and looked up into the august countenance of the venerable statesman out of his liquid, sad, and knowing eyes, and buttoned up his lips. The marquis saw them being firmly pressed together, remembered that Mrs. Harris had told him about little Henry's disinclination for speech, and knew that there would be no help forthcoming there. Also, the wait between the asking of the ques- 77 tion and the time when he had to reply was waxing heavy and intolerable; it was becoming absolutely necessary to say something.

The marquis cleared his throat. "He—he is my grandson," he said.

For some unknown reason, but characteristic of some press conferences, this statement appeared to create a sensation. "Say, it's his grandson!" "Did you hear that—it's his grandson." "What do you know, it's his grandson!" Notebooks appeared, memos were scribbled, while the photographers now surged forward shouting their own war cries as their flash lamps began to go off in the faces of their victims, blinding the marquis and confusing him even more. "Hold it, Ambassador." "Look this way, Marquis." "Put your arm around the kid, Marquis." "Hey, kid, move up to your grandpa—closer, closer." "Give us a smile now. That's it." "Just one more! Just one more!" "Put your arm around his neck, son!" "Get up on his lap, bub." "How about giving him a big kiss?"

Added to this bedlam were the further questions engendered by the revelation that the French ambassador had a member of his family traveling with him. "What's his name?" "Whose kid is he?" "Where's he going?"

The marquis found himself caught up in them. "His name is Henry."

"Henry! Henry or Henri? Is he French or English?"

The marquis was aware that sometime, somewhere, little Henry would have to open his mouth, and so he replied, "English."

The press conference now had settled down into some kind of semblance of order, and a man in the rear of the room arose and, speaking with the British accent natural to the correspondent of the London *Daily Mail,* asked, "Would that be Lord Dartington's son, Your Excellency?" As a good English reporter, he was up on his Burke's Peerage and knew that one of the daughters of the Marquis de Chassagne had married Lord Dartington of Stowe.

Diplomats ordinarily are supposed never to become flustered, and in the conduct of his official life the marquis had ice water in his veins, but this time it was a little too much and too unexpected, and the disaster engulfing him too unforeseen and unprepared for.

To tell the truth was, of course, utterly unthinkable. To reply "No" would lead to further embarrassing questions, and so without reflecting further the marquis said, "Yes, yes." All he wished for now was to conclude this ordeal as quickly as possible and reach the friendly shelter of the shed on the pier, where Mrs. Harris had promised to come and relieve him of the now embarrassing presence of little Henry.

But this latest revelation caused even a greater sensation, and once again the photographers surged forward, their flash lamps winking and flaring, while the shouts of the cameramen rose to a new pitch: "What did he say?" "He's the son of a lord?" "That makes him a dook, don't it?"

"Brother, are you a dumb cluck? That makes him a sir. Only relations of the Queen are dooks."

"What's that?" somebody said. "He's related to the Queen?" "Hey, Dook, look this way!" "Give us a smile, Lord." "What's his name—Bedlington?" "How about you giving the marquis the high sign?"

Beneath his dignified exterior the marquis broke into a cold 79 sweat at the horror of the thought that now that the press had him indissolubly linked by blood with little Henry it was not going to be quite so simple for these ties to be severed on the pier when Mrs. Harris came to collect him.

The reporters and radio men now crowded about urging, "O.K., Henry, how about saying something?" "Are you going to go to school here?" "Are you going to learn to play baseball?" "Have you got a message for American youth?" "Give us your impressions of America." "Where does your daddy live—in a castle?"

To this barrage little Henry remained mute and kept intact his reputation for taciturnity. The interviewers became more and more urgent, and little Henry's silence thicker and thicker. Finally one impatient inquisitor said facetiously, "What's the matter—has the cat got your tongue? I don't believe the marquis is your granddaddy at all."

Thereupon little Henry unbuttoned his lips. The veracity of his benefactor was being impugned. The nice bloke with the white hair and kind eyes had told a whopping big lie for him, and now corroboration was being demanded for that lie. As Mrs. Harris had said, little Henry was always one to back up a pal.

From the unbuttoned lips, in the expected childish treble, came the words, "You're bloody well right 'e's me grandfather."

In the back of the room, the eyebrows of the correspondent of the *Daily Mail* were elevated clear up to the ceiling.

The marquis felt himself engulfed in a wave of horror. He did not know that the catastrophe was just beginning to warm up.

Twelve Back in tourist class, all packed and gussied up in their best clothes, their passports and vaccination certificates clutched in their hands, Ada Harris and Mrs. Butterfield stood on deck by the rail, thrilled with their first real look at this new and exciting land, and gazed down upon the bustle of tugs, cutters, and small boats crowding around the gangways of the *Ville de Paris.*

Earlier in the morning little Henry had been escorted forward to the cabin of the marquis, his head filled with instructions to cover every possible contingency, should Mrs. Harris be delayed, etc.

Mrs. Harris was triumphant, Mrs. Butterfield nervous and perspiring now that action was again demanded of them and another crisis to be faced. She said, "Ow, Ada, are you sure it'll be all right? I've got a feeling in me bones somefink 'orrible is going to 'appen."

Even if Mrs. Harris had been able to avail herself of the prophetic nature of Mrs. Butterfield's skeleton, it was anyway too late now to alter the plan, and whilst she was not entirely at her ease with little 'Enry away from her side— during the five days on the ship she had become more than ever attached to him—she refused to be depressed. Nevertheless, just to make sure she went over the planned routine.

She said to her friend, "Come on, love, buck up and keep your hair on—what's to go wrong?" She ticked off the sequence on each finger of her hands: " 'E goes through with the marquis, no questions asked. Once he's on the pier 'e goes and stands under the letter 'B'—'B' for Brown—where we collect him. There'll be a taxi for us. 'Enry plays the standing-next-to-somebody-else game until the Schreibers have gone off. 81

Then 'e gets in with us. We've got the address. When we get there he stands down on the pavement until we 'ave a look about. When the coast's clear we'll have 'im upstairs with us as quick as wink. Didn't Mrs. Schreiber say there was enough room in the flat for a regiment to get lost in? It'll only be a couple of days 'til we find 'is dad, and then Bob's yer uncle. Garn now and forget it, and enjoy yerself. What's to go wrong?"

"Somefink," said Mrs. Butterfield firmly.

Looking down over the side and a little before them, they could see a gleaming white U. S. Coast Guard cutter with a three-inch gun mounted forward, radar mast, and huge American flag. She was connected by a gangway to an opening low in the side of the ocean liner, and as the two women watched, obviously something of importance was about to take place, for the musicians aft pulled themselves together at the behest of their leader, a guard of sailors and marines ranged themselves at the gangway in charge of a much beribboned officer, the band leader raised his arms, the officer shouted a command, rifle bolts clicked, arms were presented, the band leader's baton descended, the band crashed into "The Star-Spangled Banner," to be followed by the stirring strains of "The Stars and Stripes Forever."

To this rousing Sousa march there appeared a procession of gold-braided and uniformed aides provided by the Army, the Navy, and the Air Force, followed by dignitaries in striped trousers, frock coats, and top hats, all emerging from the hole in the side of the *Ville de Paris* and marching down the gangplank onto the cutter. Then came a momentary pause, the band leader again raised his arms and brought them down violently, and his musicians dutifully and loudly went into a

rendition of the "*Marseillaise*." The figure of a handsome, erect, and elegant old man likewise in striped trousers, gray frock coat, and gray top hat—an old man with white hair and mustache and piercing blue eyes under tufted eyebrows, the rosette of a chevalier of the Legion of Honor in his buttonhole—appeared at the exit and stood there for a moment, removing his hat and holding it against his chest during the playing of the French anthem.

"It's me friend—it's the marquis!" said Mrs. Harris, not yet aware of what was happening.

Not so Mrs. Butterfield, for as the anthem ended and to the strains of another tune the marquis marched down the gangway, the stout woman uttered a piercing scream and pointed a fat and shaking finger. "Look," she cried, "it's little 'Enry—'e's going wiv 'im!"

He was, too. His hand clutched firmly in that of the immaculately uniformed Bayswater, and followed by secretary and valet and lesser members of the embassy entourage, little Henry was following the marquis down the incline and onto the cutter, where he likewise graciously accepted the presented arms of the marine honor guard.

With a sinking sensation in her stomach, Mrs. Harris began to twig what was happening. Just before they stepped onto the cutter, Mrs. Harris saw the gray, refined face of Bayswater looking up and anxiously scanning the topside of the ship. By one of those minor miracles of communication he spotted Mrs. Harris, and for an instant their eyes met, at which point Mr. Bayswater delivered himself of a shrug which told Mrs. Harris plainer than words that he was in the grip of something bigger than himself, and was messaging his regrets.

It was indeed so. What had enmeshed Bayswater, little Henry, and the marquis was not only the high esteem in which the Marquis Hypolite de Chassagne was held personally in Washington, but that the Administration had thought it a good idea to butter up de Gaulle, who had been acting somewhat peculiar of late, by according extra honors to his ambassador and disembarking him and his entourage at Quarantine.

The marquis, his luggage, and all those with him were taken off the ship and sailed in state through the Narrows and into New York Harbor, where another honor guard awaited them at the Battery, along with a fleet of Cadillacs. They were then rolled uptown through the awesome chasm of Lower Broadway, where a small ticker-tape welcome had been organized, and bits of torn telephone books and festoons of paper ribbon covered with figures testifying to America's financial grandeur floated down upon little Henry's head. The cavalcade thereupon proceeded on across the Queensboro Bridge and out to Idlewild Airport, where the President's private aircraft, the *Columbine,* waited and the marquis and all those connected with him—with the exception of Bayswater, who remained behind to drive the Rolls down— were flown to Washington.

Little Henry went too. He had never had such a wonderful time in all his life. This was a bit of all right.

Little Henry was gone, but one could hardly say that he

was forgotten, for the afternoon papers and those of the morning following gave full coverage to the arrival of the new French ambassador and his grandson, complete with pictures of same in the various artful poses into which he had been enticed by the veteran ship news photographers—hugging his grandfather, kissing his grandfather, sitting on his grandfather's lap, or staring solemnly with his large, disturbing eyes directly into the camera.

The austere *Times* reported Henry's presence with a single line in which it said that the marquis was accompanied by his grandson, the Honorable Henry Dartington, younger son of Lord Dartington of Stowe, but the other newspapers, particularly those employing female feature writers, did some embroidery upon the story: "The handsome, white-haired, still virile French ambassador, who caused many feminine hearts to beat faster during the voyage, brought along his little grandson, Lord Henry Dartington, who is related to the Queen of England.

"Lord Dartington, who is on holiday here from Eton, where he is reported to be an Honor Student, said, 'I have brought a message from the youth of England to the youth of America—us kids must stick together. If we do not swim together we will sink. Everyone ought to learn to swim.' He said the thing he wanted to see most in America was a baseball game, and will attend the Yankee-Red Sox game at the Yankee Stadium this afternoon."

In the penthouse at number 650 Park Avenue, Mrs. Schreiber (and in the kitchen Mrs. Harris and Mrs. Butterfield too) looked at these photographs and read the stories 86 with her eyes popping.

"My goodness," she said, "so young, and a real lord already. And it says here he's a relation of the Queen. And we were on the same ship. What a nice-looking little boy—and what beautiful eyes. He's a real little gentleman, isn't he? You can take one look and tell he's an aristocrat. When the family's good, everything's good." Then her eyes met those of her husband, and they were caught there for a moment, and each knew of what the other was thinking.

To break the spell Mr. Schreiber said quickly, "I don't remember seeing him on the ship. That's a good picture of you, Henrietta—but I look like my own grandfather," for they too had been photographed by the press and appeared amongst the arrivals of importance in the SS *Ville de Paris.*

And in the vast kitchen of the penthouse, surrounded by the newspapers, from the front pages of which the promoted little Henry stared up at them, Mrs. Butterfield dithered and blubbered. "What are you going to do now? I told yer somefink was going to 'appen."

For once Mrs. Harris did not have an answer. She said,"I'm blowed if I know, Vi. And you might as well know, I forgot to give Mr. Bayswater our address."

Thirteen

650 Park Avenue, New York 21, N.Y.
April 15.
Dear Marquis,

I hope this letter reaches you, as I forgot to give our address to Mr. Bayswater, and so you could not know where we are.

Mrs. Butterfield and I saw you going onto the little boat that took you off our steamer, which neither you nor I thought of and did not expect. We waved to you, but I do not think you saw us, but Mr. Bayswater and little Henry did.

We were very sorry we got you into this trouble with Henry. It was very good of you to say he was your grandson. I suppose you could not say anything else, and the pictures in the paper look very good. Ha, ha, I guess it was not such a lark after all, and we are very sorry if we caused you any trouble.

You are a very kind man and I will come and get little Henry on Saturday when Mrs. Schreiber has given me the day off. I will come on the train in the morning.

Mrs. Schreiber has a very large flat and our rooms at the back are very nice. There are five of them with two bathrooms, and we will have no trouble in keeping little Henry out of sight when I bring him back, so you do not need to worry.

I have not had much time for sightseeing yet, though I have managed to visit Woodlawn Cemetery and it is a very nice one, with very many people buried there. Mrs. Butterfield is still very nervous crossing the streets with the traffic all going the wrong side, and policemen blowing whistles at her, but the other day she went to a supermarket on Lexington Avenue to buy

*a few things for dinner and before she came away she had spent
$187 of Mrs. Schreiber's money, for she had never been in one
before and she could not stop putting things in the little basket
and wheeling them away.*

*Mrs. Butterfield joins me in sending you her kindest regards
and thanking you for your kindness and wishes me to say how
sorry she is you have had all this trouble and hopes that little
Henry has behaved himself like a little gentleman.*

*If Saturday is alright, I will be there to collect him at 1
o'clock.*

*Please give my regards to Mr. Bayswater and tell him I will
write to him and thank him myself.*

How are you getting on in the new job?

Hoping this leaves you in the pink as it does me,

Yours sincerely,
A. Harris

*French Embassy, 18 G. Street, Washington, N.10, D.C.
April 17.
Dear Mrs. Harris,*

*Your welcome letter arrived here this morning, and although
nothing would give me greater pleasure than seeing you again
next Saturday, I am afraid that collecting little Henry, unfortunately, now that I have been compelled to claim him as a
blood relative, will not be quite that simple or instantaneous.
The fact is that Henry has been an immediate success here,
not only due to the social position with which I was led to
endow him when questioned by reporters on board the ship, but
also because of his own personal magnetism. He has charmed
an ever-growing circle of acquaintances in the Corps Diplomat-* 89

ique by not only his ability to hold his tongue, but the quaint expressions which emerge when he loosens it. He is also, I am happy to note, extremely handy with his mitts, as the British would say, and has already endeared himself to our little community by hitting the son of the Krasnodarian Minister—a child as unattractive as his father—one on the nose for making disparaging remarks about Great Britain, France, and the United States.

The truth is that little Henry has been the recipient of so many invitations which we have been compelled to accept due to the identity which he has assumed, that he will not be free to return to you until a week from Thursday, or possibly the following Monday. I shall write and let you know. In the meantime, this will leave you free to pursue your search for the boy's father, and perhaps bring this little adventure of yours to a rapid and happy conclusion.

I must confess that I await with some trepidation word from my son-in-law about this newest addition to his family. I have not heard from him as yet, but have no doubt that I shall.

As for myself, I am surely not as important as I am being made to feel by the hospitable Americans, but the sensation is a pleasant one. Is this not a wonderful and warmhearted people? We English and French must cement an enduring friendship with them if the world is not to be lost.

As soon as I can extricate Henry from the social whirl into which circumstances have forced him I will notify you. In the meantime, let me know how the search for his father proceeds.

Yours,

Chassagne

NIGHT LETTER CABLEGRAM FROM STOWE-ON-DART, DEVONSHIRE.
APRIL 18.

MY DEAR HYPOLITE HAVE JUST SEEN WIRE PHOTO AND STORIES IN
AMERICAN PRESS ON CHILD YOU HAVE SO BLITHELY KISSED OFF AS
MINE STOP ARE YOU NOT A LITTLE ASHAMED AT YOUR AGE QUES-
TION MARK NEVER MIND THOUGH THESE WORDS ARE DICTATED OUT
OF ENVY IN THE HOPE WHEN I REACH YOUR YEARS I SHALL BE ABLE
TO ACHIEVE THE SAME STOP THE AMERICAN PRESS HAS OUTDONE
ITSELF AND SOCIAL CIRCLES HERE ARE STIRRED BY THIS NEW
CANDIDATE FOR THE PEERAGE STOP STILL HE LOOKS A PROPER LAD
AND I AM GLAD TO HAVE HIM IN THE FAMILY STOP IF QUESTIONED
I WILL CORROBORATE YOUR UNBLUSHING WHOPPER BY SAYING HE
IS ONE OF MINE ON HOLIDAY IN THE U.S. STOP MARIETTE JOINS ME
IN SENDING CONGRATULATIONS AND THANKS FOR A MOST PAINLESS
BIRTH STOP YOURS AFFECTIONATELY   DARTINGTON

650 Park Avenue, New York 21, N.Y.
April 19.
Dear Mr. Bayswater,

*Well here I am at last, and hope you had no trouble getting
to Washington with the Rolls and everything is going well.*

*I guess you are surprised what happened to little Henry. But
it was not your fault, and I wish to thank you for your kindness
in suggesting it. I have not written to say thanks before because
there is a great deal of work to do in Mrs. Schreiber's flat. The
last person to live here, or whoever cleaned up was a proper pig,
or did not know anything, and what it needs is a thorough
scrubbing, which we are doing.*

91

New York is a most interesting city once you get used to the tall buildings and everyone rushing about, and they have the most wonderful cleansers in the supermarket. One is called Zip. You only put a few drops in water and it will take the paint off anything. They also have a most superior dish powder, it is called Swoosh and is better than anything we have over there. They also have a very good floor polish. It is called Swizz. You just put it on and then everything is like a skating rink. Mrs. Butterfield nearly went A. over tip after I had put some on the kitchen floor and does not think much of it.

Everything is done by electricity here, but if you want to clean a house good and proper there is nothing like bucket and soap and getting down on your hands and knees, which we are doing.

I think America is very interesting, but I am working hard and sometimes wish I was back with you all having a port and lemon on the good old Vile de Paris. Have you heard from the Tidders? I had a postcard from them from Dayton, Ohio, and have written to them to keep an eye out for George Brown, little Henry's father. The Marquis says Henry is fine, but I am glad that you are there to keep an eye on him too until I come to get him.

Well cheerio and hoping this leaves you in the pink as it does me.

I am your friend,
A. Harris

French Embassy, 18 G. Street, Washington, N.10, D.C.
April 22.
Dear Mrs. Harris,

I thank you for yours of the 19th inst. and hasten to assure you that I encountered no difficulties whatsoever on the trip down from New York to Washington, nor, might I add, had I anticipated any in a Rolls of my own selection. I am, however, not quite certain that American air is quite as salubrious for the carburetors as British air, for which they were intended, and I may have to make some adjustments later to compensate for this. You will be interested to learn, however, as I was, that the engine thermostat has not been at all affected by the American atmosphere and maintains its proper minimum coolant temperature of approximately 78° centigrade. I am forced to confess that American road surfaces are far superior to ours, and I am wondering whether the front suspension springs and rear hydraulic shock dampers cannot be somewhat released.

As it deserves, the car attracts a good deal of attention on the road, and when I stopped for petrol in the vicinity of Baltimore, a large crowd gathered to admire it and there were many exclamations of admiration. One gentleman stepped up to the car, thumped its side, and exclaimed in the American vernacular, "Boy, they know how to build 'em over there." Outside of finger marks the car came to no harm through this, and it was encouraging to me to find at least one American aware of the superiority of British craftsmanship.

I have indeed heard from Mr. and Mrs. Tidder—a letter in fact containing a photograph of their grandchild, an infant whose finer points are bound to escape one who has been a bachelor all his life.

The days aboard the SS Ville de Paris *were, as you say, most pleasant, and I look back upon them with pleasure.*

I regret the unexpected turn taken by our little scheme, but can assure you that the boy is flourishing. He has made many friends amongst the younger members of the diplomatic colony here and I will add that so far, for reasons which we will not discuss, but which are known to us both, I have managed to keep him away from the children of the British embassy, thus preserving his incognito

Please remember me kindly to Mrs. Butterfield, and with regards to your goodself,

I remain,

> *Yours faithfully,*
> *John Bayswater*

Hotel Slade, Kenosha, Wisconsin
May 1.
Dear Marquis,

I guess you will be surprised to receive a letter from me here where I have come to find the father of little Henry.

Kenosha is a beautiful city with many factories of all kinds and many parks and nice streets and houses on the shore of Lake Michigan. Mrs. Schreiber was very kind and advanced me the money to fly here when I told her I had a relative, which is only half a fib because it almost would have been wouldn't it?

I had no trouble finding Mr. George Brown and his wife here, the one from the newspaper cutting I told you about, and they were very nice to me and gave me tea, which Mr. Brown learned to drink when he was in England stationed quite close to London, and was glad when I showed him how to make it the proper English way. He had some friends who lived in Battersea so we had a good time talking over all the old places. He and his wife very kindly showed me around Kenosha in their car.

Kenosha seems to have almost as many factories as London, but Mr. Brown said it was only a small city compared to some others like Chicago and Milwaukee. The captain of the aeroplane pointed out those cities when we flew over them. They are very large.

Well, I have saved my piece of news for the last. Mr. George Brown of Kenosha, Wisconsin is not the George Brown who is the father of little Henry. He is someone else. But he was very kind about it and seemed to be very sorry he could not help me. He did not know the other George Brown, but said there were a great many in the Air Force, and he personally was acquainted with two but they were not married with anyone.

However, never you mind whether it was the right Mr. Brown or not, that is my worry and I will find him very soon or my name is not Ada Harris. In the meantime thank you for telling me I may collect him on Sunday next. I will tell Mrs. Schreiber I have a relative at Washington too. Ha ha. Having been with little Henry so long you almost are.

Now I must close as Mr. and Mrs. Brown are very kindly taking me to the airport in their car and I will go back to New York but next Sunday I will come and collect little Henry and thank you for your kindness.

Hoping this finds you in good spirits.

Yours faithfully,
Ada Harris

French Embassy, 18 G. Street, Washington, N.10, D.C.
May 4.
Dear Mrs. Harris,

Thank you so very much for your letter from Kenosha, Wisconsin, and I sympathize with you in your disappointment that the George Brown you were so certain was little Henry's father turned out to be someone else.

Nothing would have given me greater pleasure than to have received you next Sunday and to have heard personally from you your impressions of the Middle West, but alas, I fear that Fate has taken an unexpected hand and your visit must be once more postponed. It appears that little Henry has suddenly contracted a disease called the chicken pox, to which I understand children of his age are frequently addicted, and he is compelled to remain in bed, where I assure you he is receiving the very best of care, and the doctor informs me that his recovery is not far distant.

You need not be alarmed over the fact that I myself have acquired a mild attack of the disease from little Henry, who, I suspect, received it as a gift from the son of the ambassador of Persia, and thus I am sharing the quarantine. It seems the illness skipped me when I was a child. I have no complaint to make about this state of affairs, since it has given me some necessary solitude and time to reflect upon the grandeur of this vast nation and the responsibilities of my position. It will also provide you with the necessary leeway to pursue your inquiries and discover the father of this child, a task to which I have no doubt you are entirely equal.

As soon as little Henry's period of confinement is at an end I will advise you. At that time, too, I shall spread the word that the Easter holidays of my little grandson have come to an end and I have had to return him to his family in England. He will be greatly missed by the many friends he has made during his brief stay here, but by none more than the estimable Bayswater and myself. To avoid putting you to further expense in this unselfish and charitable enterprise of yours, I have commissioned Bayswater to drive you and the boy back to New York from Washington. It will also give you an opportunity to see a little more of this magnificent country.

If there is anything further I can do to aid you in your quest, do not hesitate to let me know. However, knowing you, your energy and intelligence, I have no doubt but that you will discover the right Mr. Brown.

With kind regards and wishes for good luck,

I am yours, as ever,
Chassagne

Fourteen   But if the marquis had no doubts about Mrs. Harris's ability to locate the missing father, Mrs. Harris, now that she was there, was beginning to entertain some herself, since the one man upon whom she had banked so heavily proved to be the wrong one.

Using her Cockney shrewdness and wit, she had had no difficulty locating a particular Mr. George Brown of Kenosha, Wisconsin, referred to in the newspaper cutting, and who had turned out to be the wrong one; to find the right one amidst the teeming millions who inhabited this vast land mass, so   97 great that not even the fastest jet planes could reduce it appreciably in size, was a very different matter. She discovered for instance, to her horror, that there were no less than thirty-seven George Browns in the Manhattan telephone book alone, with an equal number in Brooklyn, and further specimens crowding the other three boroughs. Just to name a few of the large cities with whose names she was now becoming familiar, there would be as many in Chicago, Detroit, Los Angeles, San Francisco, Philadelphia, and New Orleans, besides which she had no assurance whatsoever that George Brown lived in any of these cities; he might be a wealthy tobacco planter in the South, a textile merchant in New England, or a mine owner in the Far West. A letter written to the Air Force brought the reply that there had been some 453 George Browns on its roster at one time or another, and which one did she mean, where had he been stationed when, and what had been his serial number?

For the first time Mrs. Harris became fully aware of the enormity of her task, as well as the realization that she had let her romantic nature betray her into doing something not at all characteristic of a sensible London char, and that was to go off half-cocked, saddling herself in a strange land—or at least she would be saddled when she collected him from the marquis —with a small boy whom she would be forced to conceal from her kindly employers.

The almost fortuitous visitation of the chicken pox, it was true, would give her more time and breathing space before she had to face the problem of how to conceal little Henry in a penthouse apartment day and night, but for the first time Mrs. Harris felt the cold wind of discouragement.

Yet she did not give way to despondency, but remained her cheerful self and did her work as well. Under her aegis the running of the Schreiber penthouse was going well, Mrs. Butterfield, relieved of her fears and tremors by the continued absence of little Henry, was cooking like an angel, other servants were being added to the staff, with Mrs. Harris inculcating into them her own ideas of how a house ought to be kept clean, and Mrs. Schreiber, given confidence by the presence of Mrs. Harris, was beginning to lose her trepidation and commence those rounds of dinner parties and entertainments expected of a man in her husband's position.

In the course of the social duties connected with business and the eminence of their position at the head of one of the largest film and television studios in America, the Schreibers were called upon to cater to and entertain some genuinely appaling people, including newspaper columnists who wielded a make-or-break power over entertainment properties with multi-million-dollar investments, rock 'n' roll and hillbilly singers, crooked labor leaders who could shut down the studio unless properly buttered and kowtowed to, mad television directors whose frenetic profession kept them just one barely discernible step away from the booby hatch, morbid and neurotic authors who had to be pampered in order to produce a daily output of grist for the mills to grind, and an assortment of male and female actors, stars, glamour girls and boys.

Many of these were faces with which Mrs. Harris had long been familiar and admired only in their enlargements in the film theaters or their diminutions on the television screens, and who now sat living and in the flesh, close enough to touch, around the Schreibers' groaning board, devouring Mrs. Butter-   99 field's roast beef and Yorkshire pud and accepting service from Mrs. Ada Harris, imported from No. 5 Willis Gardens, Battersea, London, S.W. 11.

Not all of them were as dreadful as one might imagine, but the housebroken ones would appear to have been definitely in the minority.

Mrs. Harris, elegant in the black dress and white apron which Mrs. Schreiber had bought her, acted as third server upon these occasions, removing plates and passing the gravy, salad dressing, and cheese biscuits, while the temporary butler and first waitress took on the more serious work of getting the food to the ravenous maws of the illustrious free-loaders.

If Mrs. Harris could be said to have a weakness besides her romanticism, it was her affection and admiration for the people in the world of theater, film, and television. She bought and cherished the illusions they made for her lock, stock, and barrel.

Ada Harris was a moral woman, with her own rigid code of ethics and behavior, and one who would stand for no nonsense or misbehavior on the part of others. To show people, however, this strict code simply did not apply, and she acknowledged that they lived in a world of their own and were entitled to different standards. Thus, Mrs. Schreiber's Friday night dinner parties were as near heaven socially as Mrs. Harris ever expected to come. To see Gerald Gaylor, North America's great film star, on a Thursday afternoon off, his beautiful head the size of a two-story building on the Radio City Music Hall screen, and then the following Friday to see that same glamorous bean close up, and gaze upon him engulfing six martinis one after the other, was a bliss she had never expected to attain.

There was Bobby Toms, the teen-age rock 'n' roller with the curly hair and sweet face, and she closed her eyes to the fact that he got drunk early in the evening and used very bad language in the presence of ladies, language that was only surpassed by that issuing from the exquisite lips of Marcella Morell, the film ingénue, but who was so beautiful that even the most dreadful words when she used them somehow seemed beautiful too—if one had the same feeling toward show people as Mrs. Harris. There was a hillbilly singer by the name of Kentucky Claiborne, who came to dine in unwashed jeans, black leather jacket, and fingernails in deep mourning, a famous comic who actually was funny in real life as well, dancers, heavies, beautiful actresses who dressed glamorously —in short, a veritable paradise for Mrs. Harris and Mrs. Butterfield as well, who tasted the thrills of high life in the theatrical world via the reports of her friend.

However, broad-minded as she was and extraordinarily tolerant in her approach to the people of the wonderful world of entertainment, Mrs. Harris soon found the fly in this ointment —namely the hillbilly singer—who made himself so disagreeable that it was not long before he was loathed by everyone with whom he came in contact, including Mrs. Harris.

Before his first appearance at a Schreiber dinner party Mrs. Schreiber had given her something of a warning of what to expect, since the goodhearted American woman was certain that Mrs. Harris would not have encountered such a specimen in London and did not wish her to be too greatly shocked by his 101 appearance and comportment. "Mr. Claiborne is a kind of a genius," she explained. "I mean, he's the idol of the teen-agers and inclined to be a little unusual, but he is very important to my husband, who is signing him for North American Pictures and Television, and it is a great feather in his cap—everyone is after Kentucky Claiborne."

The name had already awakened memories of curiously unpleasant feelings within Mrs. Harris, recollections of emotions which eluded her until she suddenly had a moment of recall to the time when her adventure in a sense had begun; this was the night back in her little flat in London when the Gussets next door had used the caterwauling of an American hillbilly singer by that name on the wireless to cover up the beating of little Henry.

By that osmosis through which servants pick up what is going on about them, not only through their ears and the gossip of pantry, kitchen, and servants' quarters, but also somehow through the pores of their skin, Mrs. Harris acquired the information and imparted it to Mrs. Butterfield that this same Kentucky Claiborne, emerging from nowhere in the southern portion of the United States, had had a meteoric rise as a hillbilly singer, due to the fact that his recordings of folk songs had suddenly caught on with the teen-agers, instigating a competition of frantic bidding amongst the moving-picture and television powers to sign him up.

Mr. Schreiber, who in a short time had metamorphosed into a genuinely brilliant cine-mogul, had not been afraid to gamble and was far out in front in the race. His lawyers and the lawyers of Claiborne's agent, a Mr. Hyman, were in 102 the process of hammering out a contract in which the singer would be paid the sum of ten million dollars over five years —a sum so vast that not only Mrs. Harris, but all of the entertainment world, was staggered.

In the meantime it was necessary to keep Mr. Claiborne in an amiable frame of mind, which was difficult, for it was obvious even to Mrs. Harris that, celebrity or not, Kentucky Claiborne was vain, shallow, selfish, self-centered, loud, rude, insulting, a bore, and a boor. As his agent, Mr. Hyman, put it to Mr. Schreiber: "So what d'you want? He's a jerk—but he's a jerk with talent. The kids are nuts about him."

This was true, as it is of many of the repellent characters who work their way to the top in the entertainment world. Now a thirty-fiveish man with already thinning hair, deep-set eyes, and blue jowls, Kentucky Claiborne had suddenly emerged from the Deep South, where he had been moaning his hinterland folk songs in honky-tonks and cheap night clubs to the accompaniment of his guitar, to become a national sensation. His eyes, his voice, his demeanor, his delivery, apparently evoked the loneliness and melancholy of the pioneer woodsmen of America's past.

While his background and origins remained undisclosed, he must have been a poor boy—not to mention poor white trash—for the sudden access of fame, wealth, and adulation made him drunker even than he was wont to become on his favorite tipple of bourbon and branch. Added to these charms was the fact that he chewed tobacco, had grimy fingernails, and apparently did not wash either himself or his hillbilly uniform too often.

The Schreibers put up with him because they had to; their guests did because most of them were genuinely fond of the 103

Schreibers, and many of them had come from equally humble origins and somehow had adjusted themselves.

It did not take Mrs. Butterfield long to loathe Mr. Claiborne with equal fervor, since his remarks anent her cooking were delivered in a loud voice which, when the swinging doors opened, penetrated right into the kitchen, and on anything she missed Mrs. Harris indignantly filled her in.

Mr. Claiborne was vociferous and uninhibited on all subjects which in any way pertained to himself. For instance, one evening when Mrs. Butterfield had concocted a really delectable cheese soufflé, the hillbilly singer rejected it out of hand after a sniff at it, saying "Pee-yew! That smells! What Ah wouldn't give for some real old-fashioned southern cookin'— po'k-fat back with turnip greens and pot liquor, or good old southern fried chicken with hush-puppies. That's the kind of eatin' foh a man. Ah cain't put this foreign stuff in mah belly. Ah'll just hold off until you pass the meat an' potaters."

At another meal he delivered an oration on his prejudices. "Ah ain't got no time for niggers, nigger lovers, or foreigners. Ah say, ship all the niggers back where they come from, and don't let no more foreigners in. Then we'll have God's own country here sure enough."

Poor Mr. Schreiber turned quite crimson at these remarks, and some of his guests looked as though they were about to explode. However, they had all been briefed that if Mr. Claiborne were to be irritated he might suddenly break off the contract negotiations going on and take his fabulous popularity and box-office value elsewhere.

Mrs. Harris passed along her opinion of Mr. Claiborne to

Mrs. Butterfield in good, solid Battersea terms, concluding more mildly, "He looked right at me when 'e passed that remark about foreigners. It was all I could do to keep me tongue in me 'ead."

When Mr. Schreiber protested to Claiborne's agent, Mr. Hyman, and asked whether he could not exert a civilizing influence on him, at least so far as his personal appearance, tongue, and table manners were concerned, that individual replied, "What do you wanna do? He's a nature boy. That's why he's the idol of them millions of American kids. He's just like they are. Clean him up and put him in a monkey suit and you're gonna spoil him. He's gonna make plenty of dough for you, so why should you care?"

Fifteen The day dawned eventually when Mrs. Harris, notified by the marquis that little Henry was no longer catching, in fact was once more in the full flush of youthful health, boarded the *Congressional Limited* at Pennsylvania Station and took the train to Washington, where first, with her usual energy and initiative, she engaged a cab driver to take her for a quick swing around the nation's capital before depositing her at the French embassy.

After a tour which embraced the Capitol, the Washington Monument, the Lincoln Memorial, the Pentagon Unit, and the White House, the driver, who had been in the Navy during the war and spent a good deal of time in British waters and 105

British ports, leaned back and asked, "Well, Ma, what do you think of it? It ain't Buckinham Palace or Westminster Abbey —but it's our own."

"Lor' love yer, ducks," Mrs. Harris replied, "you can't have everything. It's even prettier than in the pictures."

At the embassy Mrs. Harris was greeted by the Marquis de Chassagne with great warmth—compounded in part from the genuine affection he felt for her, and in part from relief that what might have turned into a very sticky business was now happily concluded, at least so far as he was concerned.

A quite new Henry Brown came storming forth to throw his arms about the person of Mrs. Harris; new in that, as with most children bedded with chicken pox, he had grown an inch during the process, and through proper nourishment and lack of abuse had also filled out. The eyes and the large head were still wise and knowing, but had lost their sadness. Somehow he had even managed to acquire some manners by imitation, and during the luncheon treat that the marquis provided for Mrs. Harris he succeeded in refraining from bolting his food, eating with his knife, and other social misdemeanors.

Mrs. Harris, herself a great stickler for etiquette and the gracefully lifted little finger, was not insensitive to these improvements and remarked, "Lor' love yer, dearie, your father will be proud of you."

"Ah," said the marquis, "I was coming to that. Have you found him yet?"

Mrs. Harris had the grace to blush. "Blimey, no," she said, "and I ain't 'arf ashamed of meself—boasting to Mrs. Butterfield how I'd find him in half a jiffy if I ever got to America. Me and my big mouth! But I will." She turned and promised little Henry, "Don't you worry, 'Enry. I will find your dad for you, or me nyme's not Ada 'Arris."

Little Henry accepted this pledge with no particular alteration of expression or change in his taciturnity. At that moment, truth to tell, he was not especially concerned whether she did or not. Things had never been so good with him, and he was not inclined to be greedy.

The marquis accompanied them to the front door of the embassy, where the blue Rolls-Royce waited, its figurehead and chromework gleaming, with the handsome and immaculate Bayswater behind the wheel.

"Can I ride up front, Uncle Hypolite?"

"If Bayswater will permit it." The chauffeur nodded gracious acquiescence.

"Both of us—Auntie Ada too?"

To his surprise Mr. Bayswater found himself involved in a second acquiescence. Never before had anyone but a footman ridden beside him in the front seat of a Rolls.

"Good-by, Uncle Hypolite," said the boy, and went up and threw his arms about the neck of the marquis and hugged him. "You've been a real swell to me."

The marquis patted his shoulder and said, "Good-by, my little nephew and grandson. Good luck, and be a good boy." To Mrs. Harris he said, "Good-by, madame, and good luck to you too—and when you find the father I hope he will be a good man who will love him." He stood on the pavement watching them go until they turned the corner, and then went back into the embassy. He was no longer feeling relieved, but only a little lonely and a little older.

Thus, driving along the turnpike from Washington in the marquis's elegant Rolls-Royce, Bayswater, little Henry, who in a new suit and shoes purchased for him by the marquis looked more than ever like a young lordling out of the pages of the *Tatler* or the *Queen,* and Mrs. Harris sat all together up front in the chauffeur's compartment and chatted and compared notes.

Mrs. Harris thought she had never seen anyone quite as elegant or attractive as Mr. Bayswater in his gray whipcord uniform and the gray cap with the marquis's badge above the peak. Mr. Bayswater found himself somewhat unsettled by the pleasure he was taking in Mrs. Harris's company. Ordinarily on such a trip he would have listened to nothing but the gentle, almost inaudible purring of the Rolls-Royce, the whine of the tires, and the exquisite silence of the body bolts and springs. As it was, now he lent half an ear to the questions and chatter of Mrs. Harris, who was all settled into the comfortable leather seat for a proper chinwag.

He even deigned to talk to her, something he had not been known to do while driving since 1937, when he had had to speak sharply to Lord Boothey's footman sitting next to him to keep his eyes straight ahead instead of letting them wander all about. He said, "I have driven through Madison, Wisconsin, a city of wide avenues and pleasant homes, but I have never been to Kenosha. What would you say was the most attractive feature of that city?"

"Something they had in the café of the 'otel there—North Country flapjacks with little pig sausages and genu-ine maple syrup. Coo! I never ate anything so good in me life. Four

108

'elpings of them, I 'ad. Afterwards I was sick. But blimey if it wasn't worth it."

"Moderation is the signpost to health," declared Mr. Bayswater somewhat sententiously.

"Go on with you, John," said Mrs. Harris, using his Christian name for the first time. "Did you ever eat a North Country flapjack?"

After he had got over the initial shock of hearing his first name thus falling from the lips of a female of the species, Mr. Bayswater smiled a kind of a grayish, wintry smile and said, "Well, perhaps I haven't, Ada. But I'll tell you what we'll do, since you rather fancy your stomach; there's a Howard Johnson's about five miles ahead, and we'll stop off there for a snack. Did you ever eat New England clam chowder? You'll be sick again, I'll warrant. It's the best in the world. And for the nipper there's ice cream. Howard Johnson's has thirty-seven different varieties of ice cream."

"Lumme," marveled Mrs. Harris. "Thirty-seven kinds! There ain't that many flavors to make ice cream of. Would you believe that, 'Enry?"

Henry looked up at Mr. Bayswater with great trust and confidence. "If 'e says so," he replied.

They pulled up to the orange and white Howard Johnson's restaurant at the edge of the turnpike, where hundreds of cars were similarly lined up and nosed in like pigs at a trough, and there they sat and sampled Lucullan bits of American roadside gastronomy.

This time, however, it was not Mrs. Harris, but little Henry, who was sick. He had got successfully through nine 109

of the famous Howard Johnson's flavors before the tenth—
huckleberry licorice—threw him. But after he had been
cleaned up he was as good as new, and, piling back into the
Rolls-Royce, they proceeded merrily northward toward the
great metropolis on the Hudson.

On the final lap Mr. Bayswater regaled Mrs. Harris with
accounts of little Henry's popularity amongst the diplomatic
set before the chicken pox laid him low and curbed his
activities, which seemed to include running faster and leaping
and jumping farther and higher than the scions of the ambas-
sadors of Spain, Sweden, Indonesia, Ghana, Finland, and the
Low Countries.

"My word," said Mrs. Harris. And then, throwing a wink
over little Henry's head at Mr. Bayswater, said, "But 'ow
come they didn't twig that little 'Enry wasn't——I mean
——?"

"Hoh!" scoffed Mr. Bayswater. "How would they? They
can't speak the king's English any better themselves. A leader,
that's what that boy's going to be."

Little Henry here broke one of his long silences. "I liked
the Easter party on the lawn best," he confided to Mrs.
Harris. "We had to 'unt Easter eggs that was hidden, and we
had egg races on a spoon. Uncle Ike said I was the best of
anybody, and someday I'd be a champion."

"Did 'e now?" said Mrs. Harris. "That was nice. 'Oo did
you say said that—Uncle Ike? 'Oo's Uncle Ike?"

"I dunno," replied little Henry. " 'E was a kind of bald-
headed bloke, and a bit of all right. 'E knew I was from London right away."

110   "He is referring to the President of the United States and

the annual Easter party for the children of the members of the Diplomatic Corps on the White House lawn," explained Mr. Bayswater just a trifle loftily. "Mr. Eisenhower conducted the ceremonies personally. I stood that close to him meself," lapsing again at the mere memory of the event. "We exchanged a few words."

"Lor' love yer—the two of yer 'obnobbing with presidents! I once was almost close enough to the Queen to touch—Christmas shopping at 'Arrods."

The Rolls was purring—it seemed almost floating—over the steel and concrete tracery of the great Skyway over the Jersey marshes. In the distance, shining in the late afternoon spring sunshine, gleamed the turrets of Manhattan. The sun was caught by the finger tower atop the Empire State Building, glinted from the silvered steel spike terminating the Chrysler Building farther uptown, more than a thousand feet above the street level, and sometimes was caught illuminating every window of the burnished walls of the R.C.A. and other buildings in midtown New York, until they literally seemed on fire.

Mrs. Harris feasted her eyes upon the distant spectacle before they plunged into the caverns of the Lincoln Tunnel, and murmured, "Coo, and I thought the Eiffel Tower was somefink!" She was thinking, *"Who would ever have thought that Ada Harris of 5, Willis Gardens, Battersea, would be sitting in a Rolls-Royce next to such a kind and elegant gentleman, a real, proper gent—Mr. John Bayswater—looking with her own eyes upon such a sight as New York?"* And the graying little chauffer was thinking, *"Whoever would have thought that Mr. John Bayswater, of Bayswater, would be watching the ex-*

*pression of delight and joy upon the face of a little trans-
planted London char as she gazed upon one of the grandest
and most beautiful spectacles in the world, instead of keeping
both eyes on the congested road, and his ears attuned only to
the voices of his vehicle?"*

Mrs. Harris had the chauffeur drop them for safety's sake at
the corner of Madison Avenue, and as they said good-by and
she expressed her thanks for the ride and the meal, Mr. Bayswater was surprised to hear himself say, "I don't suppose
we'll be seeing you again." And then added, "Good luck
with the nipper. I hope you find his parent. You might let us
know—the marquis will be interested."

Mrs. Harris said blithely, "If you're ever up this way again,
get on the blower—Sacramento 9-9900. We might go to the
flicks at the Music 'All. It's me fyvorite plyce. Mrs. Butterfield and me go every Thursday."

"If you're ever in Washington, look us up," said Mr.
Bayswater. "The marquis will be glad to see you."

"Righty-ho." She and little Henry stood on the corner
and watched him merge into the stream of traffic. In the
Rolls, Mr. Bayswater watched the two of them in his
rear-vision mirror until he came *that* close to touching fenders
with a Yellow Cab, and the exchange of pleasantries with the
driver thereof, who called him "a Limey so-and-so," brought
him back to the world of realities and Rolls-Royces.

Mrs. Harris nipped into a drugstore and telephoned Mrs.
Butterfield to notify her of their arrival and ascertain whether
the coast was clear.

112

Sixteen The introducing of little Henry Brown into the servants' quarters of the Schreiber penthouse at 650 Park Avenue presented no problems whatsoever. Mrs. Harris simply escorted him thither through the delivery entrance on Sixty-seventh Street, up the service elevator, and through the back door of the huge flat.

Nor would keeping him there have presented any insurmountable difficulties, trained as he was to self-effacement. The Schreibers never entered the servants' quarters, they never used the back way into the apartment. There was an abundance of food at all times in the huge freezing units and iceboxes into which a child would make no appreciable dent, and since he was a silent little chap he might have gone undetected there indefinitely, but for the unfortunate effect that his presence had upon the nerves of Mrs. Butterfield.

Well accustomed by now to the ways of American supermarkets and delivery men, no longer frightened by the giantism of the city, delighted with the dollars she was amassing, Mrs. Butterfield had allowed herself to be lulled into a sense of false security by the protracted absence of little Henry amongst the diplomatic set in Washington. Now his return and physical presence on the premises put an end to that. All her fears, nervous tremors, worries, and prophecies of doom and disaster returned, and in double measure, for there now seemed no possible solution, happy ending, or, for that matter, an ending of any kind but disaster to the impasse.

With the return of Mrs. Harris from Kenosha, Wisconsin, bearing the ill tidings that this Brown was not the father of the boy, and her subsequent failure to make any progress in discovering him, Mrs. Butterfield could see only execution or dungeons and durance vile staring them in the face. They had kidnaped a child in broad daylight in the streets of London, they had stowed him away on an ocean liner without paying his fare or keep, they had smuggled him into the United States of America—a capital crime, obviously, from all the precautions taken to prevent it—and now they were compounding all previous felonies by concealing him in the home of their employers. All of this could only end in a catastrophe of cataclysmic proportions.

Unhappily, it was in her cooking that the effects of strain began to show.

Salt and sugar were frequently interchanged; syrup and vinegar got themselves mysteriously mixed; soufflés either fell flat or blew up; sauces curdled and roasts burned. Her delicate sense of timing went completely to pot so that she could no longer produce a four-minute egg that was not either raw or stone-hard. Her coffee grew watery, her toast cindery—she could not even make an honest British cup of tea any more.

As for the state banquets she was called upon to prepare for the entertainment of Mr. Schreiber's celebrated employees, they beggared description, and people who once were eager to be asked to one of the Schreiber evenings now invented every kind of excuse to absent themselves from the horrors that appeared from Mrs. Butterfield's kitchen.

Nor was it any satisfaction to Mrs. Schreiber, to Mrs. Harris, or to Mrs. Butterfield that the only one who now seemed contented was Kentucky Claiborne, who, when a particularly charred roast accompanied by a quite appallingly oversalted and overthickened gravy appeared on the table, dug into it with both elbows flying, and bawled, "Say, Henrietta, this is   115 more like it. Ah reckon you must have fired that old bag you had in the kitchen and got yourself a hundred per cent American cook. Ah'll just have some more of that there spoon gravy."

Naturally, all this did not happen at once. It was a more gradual deterioration than as narrated, but with a sudden acceleration as Mrs. Butterfield, herself aware of her sins of omission and commission, grew only the more nervous and upset, and of course from then on things worsened rapidly, until Mr. Schreiber was called upon to ask his wife, "See here, Henrietta, what's got into that pair you dragged over here from London? We ain't had a decent meal in two weeks. How am I going to ask anybody here for dinner any more?"

Mrs. Schreiber said, "But everything was going along so fine at first—and she seemed to be such a wonderful cook."

"Well, she ain't now," said Mr. Schreiber. "And if I were you I'd get her out of here before she poisons someone."

Mrs. Schreiber pressed Mrs. Harris on the subject, and for the first time found the little charwoman, of whom she was genuinely fond, not entirely co-operative. When she asked, "Tell me, Mrs. Harris, is anything wrong with Mrs. Butterfield?" she got only a curious look and a reply, " 'Oo, Violet? Not 'er. Violet's one of the best."

Mrs. Harris herself was in a fearful dilemma, torn between affection for and loyalty to her kind employer, and love and even greater loyalty to her lifelong friend, who she knew was making a walloping ball-up of her job, and likewise why. What was she to do, besides what she had been doing, which was to implore Mrs. Butterfield to pull herself together, only 116 to be deluged by a flood of reproaches for the fix they were in, and predictions of swift retribution? She herself had not been blind to the deterioration in Mrs. Butterfield's art, and the dissatisfaction at the table, and was aware now of a new danger that threatened them, namely that Mr. Schreiber would order them both deported to London. If this happened before the finding of little Henry's father, then they were really for it, for Mrs. Harris had no illusions about being able to smuggle him back as they had brought him over. Such a caper would work once, but never twice.

Mrs. Harris knew that she had erred in not taking Mrs. Schreiber into her confidence immediately, and it flustered her to the point where she did the wrong thing. On top of giving Mrs. Schreiber a short and unsatisfactory answer, she then went out for a walk on Park Avenue to try to think things out and keep the situation from deteriorating still further.

Thus she was not present when for the first time Mrs. Schreiber invaded the labyrinth of her own servants' quarters to have a heart-to-heart talk with Mrs. Butterfield, and if possible ascertain the psychological causes for her difficulties, and discovered little Henry in the servants' sitting room, silently and happily packing away his five o'clock tiffin.

Mild surprise turned into genuine shock when suddenly Mrs. Schreiber recognized him from all the photographs she had seen in the newspapers, and cried, "Great heavens, it's the duke! I mean, the marquis—I mean the grandson of the French ambassador. What on earth is he doing here?"

Even though this catastrophal bolt of lightning had been long awaited by Mrs. Butterfield, her reaction to it was what might have been expected: she fell upon her knees with her hands clasped, crying, "Oh Lor', ma'am, don't send us to jyle!   117

I'm only a poor widow with but a few more years to live." And thereafter her sobs and weeping became so loud and uncontrollable that they penetrated into the front of the flat and brought Mr. Schreiber hurrying to the scene.

For the first time, even little Henry lost some of his aplomb at seeing one of his protectresses reduced to a hysterical jelly, and he himself burst into wails of terror.

It was upon this tableau that Mrs. Harris entered as she returned from her little promenade. She stood in the doorway for a moment contemplating the scene. "Oh blimey," she said. "Aren't we for it now."

Mr. Schreiber was also staggered at finding in a state bordering upon hysteria his Cockney cook, plus a young boy whose image not so long ago had decorated the front pages of the metropolitan press as the son of a lord and the grandson of the French ambassador to the United States.

Somehow, perhaps because she was the only member of the drama who seemed to be at all calm and collected, he had a feeling that Mrs. Harris might be at the bottom of this. Actually, at this point, contemplating the scene and aware of all its implications, the little char was doing her best to suppress a giggle. Her eyes were shining with wicked merriment and inner mirth, for she was of the breed that never cries over spilt milk —to the contrary, is more likely to laugh at it if there is a joke to be found. She had always known that eventually they must be caught, and now that it had happened she had no intention of panicking.

"Can you explain this, Mrs. Harris?" Mr. Schreiber demanded. "You seem to be the only one left here with any wits about her. What the devil is the grandson of the French ambassador doing here? And what's got into Mrs. Butterfield?"

"That's just what's the matter," Mrs. Harris replied. "'E ain't the grandson of the marquis. That's what's got into 'er cooking. Poor thing, 'er nerves 'ave went." She then addressed herself to the child and her friend, saying, "'Ere, 'ere, 'Enry, stop yer bawling. Come on, Vi—pull yourself together."

Thus admonished, both of them ceased their outcries instantly. Little Henry returned to his victuals, while Mrs. Butterfield hauled herself to her feet and mopped her eyes with her apron.

"There now," said Mrs. Harris, "that's better. Now maybe I'd better explain. This is little 'Enry Brown. He's a orphan, sort of. We brought 'im over with us from London to help 'im find 'is father."

It was now Mr. Schreiber's turn to look bewildered. "Oh, come on, Mrs. Harris, this is the same kid whose picture was in the paper as the grandson of the marquis."

Mrs. Schreiber said, "I remarked at the time what a nice little boy he seemed to be."

"That's because the marquis took 'im through the Immigrytion for us," elucidated Mrs. Harris. "Otherwise they wouldn't have let 'im in. The marquis had to say something, so 'e used his nut. The marquis is an old friend of mine— little 'Enry's been 'avin' the chicken pox with him."

Mr. Schreiber's already slightly prominent eyes threatened to pop out of his head as he gasped, "The marquis smuggled him through for you? Do you mean to say——?"

"Maybe I better explyne," said Mrs. Harris, and forthwith 119 and with no further interruptions she launched into the story of little Henry, the lost GI father, the Gussets, and all that had taken place, including the abortive and unsuccessful visit to Kenosha, Wisconsin. "And of course that's why poor Vi got so nervous 'er cooking went orf. There's none better than Vi when she's got nuffink on 'er mind."

Mr. Schreiber suddenly sat down in a chair and began to roar with laughter until the tears ran down his cheeks, while Mrs. Schreiber went over, put her arms around little Henry, and said, "You poor dear. How very brave of you. You must have been terrified."

In one of his rare moments of loquacity and warmth, and sparked by Mrs. Schreiber's cuddle, little Henry said, "Who —me? What of?"

Mr. Schreiber recovered sufficiently to say, "And if that ain't the damnedest thing I ever heard of! The French ambassador stuck with the kid and has to say it's his grandson. You know you could have got into serious trouble with this, don't you? And still can if they find out about the kid."

"That's what I've been lying awake nights thinking about," confessed Mrs. Harris. "It would have been easy as wink if that Mr. Brown at Kenosha had been 'is father—a father's got the right to have 'is own son in 'is own country, ain't 'e? But he wasn't."

"Well, what are you going to do now?" asked Mr. Schreiber.

Mrs. Harris looked at him gloomily and did not reply, for the simple reason that she did not know.

"Why can't he stay here with us until Mrs. Harris locates his father?" said Mrs. Schreiber, and gave the child another hug, and received one in return—a sudden outburst of spontaneous affection which thrilled her heart. "Nobody need know. He's such a dear little boy."

Mrs. Butterfield waddled over to Mrs. Schreiber, twisting a corner of her apron. "Oh, ma'am, if you only could," she said. "I'd cook me 'eart out for yer."

Mr. Schreiber, whose face had been expressing considerable doubts as to the wisdom of such a course, brightened visibly as at least one solution to what had become a problem dawned, and said to Henry, "Come here, sonny." The boy arose, went over, and stood in front of the seat of Mr. Schreiber and looked him straight and unabashedly in the eye.

"How old are you, sonny?"

"Eight, sir."

"Sir! That's a good beginning. Where did you learn that?"

"Auntie Ada taught me."

"So you can learn? That's good. Are you glad Mrs. Harris brought you away from London?"

With his large eyes bent upon Mr. Schreiber little Henry breathed a heartfelt sigh and replied, "Not 'arf."

"Would you like to live in America?"

Little Henry had the right answer here too. "Cor'," he said. "'Oo wouldn't?"

"Do you think you could learn to play baseball?"

Apparently little Henry had been experimenting in Washington. "Ho," he scoffed. "Anybody who can play cricket can 'it a baseball. I knocked one for six—only you call it a 'ome run 'ere."

"Say," said Mr. Schreiber, now genuinely interested, "that's good. Maybe we can make a ball player out of him."

It had taken slightly longer, but there was that wonderful   121 pronoun "we" again. Mr. Schreiber had become a member of the firm. He said to the boy, "What about your father? I guess you're pretty anxious to find him, eh?"

To this little Henry did not reply, but stood there silently regarding Mr. Schreiber out of eyes that only shortly before then had reflected little else than misery and unhappiness. Since he had never known a real father he could not genuinely form a concept of what one would be like, except that if it was anything like Mr. Gusset he would rather not. Still, everybody was making such a fuss and trying so hard to find this parent that he felt he had best not be impolite on the subject, so instead of answering the question he said, finally, "You're O.K., guv'ner. I like you."

Mr. Schreiber's round face flushed with pleasure, and he patted the boy on the shoulder. "Well, well," he said. "We'll have to see what we can do. In the meantime you can stay here with Mrs. Harris and Mrs. Butterfield." He turned to Mrs. Harris. "Just how far have you got locating the boy's father?"

Mrs. Harris told him how, foolishly, Mr. Brown of Kenosha, Wisconsin, had been all the eggs in her basket, and now that they had been broken, she was at a loss as to how to continue. She showed him her official letter from the Air Force demanding to know which George Brown she referred to of the 453 who at one time or another had been in the service, and asking to know his birthplace, birthday, serial number, date of enlistment, date of discharge, places of service abroad, at home, etc.

Mr. Schreiber looked at the formidable document and

scoffed, "Huh, those guys couldn't find anyone if he was right under their noses. Just you leave it to me. I got a real organization. We got distribution branches in every big city in the U.S.A. If we can't turn him up for you, nobody can. What did you say his name was? And have you got any other dope on him—where he was stationed, maybe, or how old he was at the time of his marriage, or any other thing that would help us?"

Mrs. Harris shamefacedly had to admit that she could offer no more than that his name was George Brown, he had been an American airman stationed at an American air base in England sometime in 1950, and that he had married a waitress by the name of Pansy Cott, who had borne him little Henry, refused to accompany him to America, was divorced by Mr. Brown, had remarried, and vanished. As she revealed the paucity of these details, Mrs. Harris became even more aware and further ashamed of the manner in which she had let her enthusiasm carry her away and handled the affair. "Lumme," she said. "I've played the fool, 'aven't I? Wicked, that's what I've been. If I was you I'd send us all packing and 'ave done with it."

Mrs. Schreiber protested, "I think what you've done is absolutely wonderful, Mrs. Harris. Don't you think so, Joel? Nobody else could have."

Mr. Schreiber made a small movement of his head and shoulders which indicated a doubtful but not antagonistic "Well" and then said, "Sure ain't much to go on, is there? But if anyone can find this feller, our organization can." To little Henry he said, "O.K., sonny. Tomorrow is Sunday. We'll   123 get a baseball bat, ball, and glove and go in Central Park and see if you can hit a home run off me. I used to be a pretty good pitcher when I was a kid."

Seventeen   It was shortly before one of Mrs. Schreiber's social-business dinners that Kentucky Claiborne definitely set the cap onto the loathing that Mrs. Harris had come to entertain for him and made it an undying and implacable affair.

He had arrived, as usual, unkempt and unwashed in his blue jeans, cowboy boots, and too-fragrant leather jacket, but this time he had turned up an hour before the scheduled time, and for two reasons: one was that he liked to tank up early before the drinks were slowed down to being passed one at a time, and the other was that he wished to tune up his guitar at the Schreiber piano, for Mr. Schreiber was entertaining some important distributors and heads of television networks and had persuaded Kentucky to sing after supper.

Kentucky was a bourbon-and-branch man, and very little of the latter. After four tumblerfuls of "Old Grandpappy" that were more than half neat, he tuned up his instrument, twanging a half a dozen chords, and launched into a ballad of love and death amongst the feudin' Hatfields and McCoys. Halfway through he looked up to find himself being stared at by a small boy with a slightly too-large head and large, interested, and intelligent eyes.

124   Kentucky paused in the midst of the blow-down of a whole

passel of Hatfields at the hands of McCoys and their rifles and said, "Beat it, bub."

Little Henry, surprised rather than hurt, said, "What for? Why can't I stay 'ere and listen?"

"Because I said beat it, bub, that's why." And then, as his ear suddenly reminded him of something, he said, "Say, ain't that Limey talk? Are you a Limey?"

Little Henry knew well enough what a Limey was, and was proud of it. He looked Kentucky Claiborne in the eye and said, "You're bloody well right I am—and what's it to you?"

"What's it to me?" said Kentucky Claiborne with what little Henry should have recognized as a dangerous amiability. "Why, it's just that if there's anything I hate worse than nigger talk, it's Limey talk. And if there's anything I hate more than niggers, it's Limeys. I told you to beat it, bub," and he thereupon leaned over and slapped little Henry on the side of the head hard, sending him spinning. Almost by reflex little Henry released his old-time Gusset wail, and instinctively, to drown out the sound, Kentucky launched into the next stanza in which avenging Hatfields now slaughtered McCoys.

And in the pantry where Mrs. Harris was helping to lay out canapés the little char could hardly believe her ears, and for a moment she thought that she was back in her own flat at No. 5 Willis Gardens, Battersea, listening to the wireless and having tea with Mrs. Butterfield, for penetrating to her ears had been the caterwauling of Kentucky Claiborne, then a thump and the sound of a blow, the wailing of a hurt child, followed by music up *forte crescendo*. Then she realized where she actually was, and what must have happened, though she

126

could not believe it, and went charging out of the pantry and into the music room to find a weeping Henry with one side of his face scarlet from the blow, and a laughing Kentucky Claiborne twanging his guitar.

He stopped when he saw Mrs. Harris and said, "Ah tol' the little bastard to beat it, but he's got wax in his ears, so Ah had to clout him one. Git him out of here—Ah'm practicin'."

"Bloody everything!" raged Mrs. Harris. And then picturesquely added thereto, "You filthy brute, to strike a 'armless child. You touch 'im again and I'll scratch yer eyes out."

Kentucky smiled his quiet, dangerous smile, and took hold of his instrument by the neck with both hands. "Goddam," he said. "If this house just ain't filled with Limeys. Ah just tol' this kid if there's anything Ah hates worse'n a nigger it's a Limey. Git outta here before I bust this geetar over yoh' haid."

Mrs. Harris was no coward, but neither was she a fool. In her varied life in London she had come up against plenty of drunks, ruffians, and bad actors, and she knew a dangerous man when she saw one. Therefore, she used her common sense, collected little Henry to her, and went out.

Once in the safety of the servants' quarters she soothed him, bathed his face in cold water, and said, "There, there, dearie, never you mind that brute. Ada 'Arris never forgets. It may take a week, it may take a month, it may take a year—but we'll pay 'im orf for that. 'Ittin' a defenseless child for being English!"

Had Mrs. Harris kept a ledger on her vendettas it would have been noted that there were none that had not been liquidated long before the time she had allotted. Kentucky

Claiborne had got himself into her black book, for, in Mrs. Harris's opinion, the crime unpardonable, and he was going to pay for it—somehow, sometime. His goose was as good as cooked.

Eighteen Up to this time, due to business in hand, worry over little Henry and the marquis, and the exigencies of her duties, namely to help Mrs. Schreiber put her house in order and get it running properly. Mrs. Harris's vista of New York after those two breath-taking approaches was limited to the broad valley of Park Avenue with its towering apartment houses on either side and the endless two-way stream of traffic obeying the stop and go of the red and green lights day and night. That, with the shops a block east on Lexington Avenue, and a few trips to Radio City Music Hall with Mrs. Butterfield had been the extent of her contact with Manhattan.

Because she was busy and preoccupied, and everything was so changed and different from what she had been accustomed to, she had not yet had time to be overwhelmed by it. But now all this was to be altered. It was the George Browns who were to introduce Mrs. Harris to that incredible Babylon and metropolis known as Greater New York.

It came about through the fact that there was now an interim period of comparative peace, with little Henry integrated into the servants' quarters of the penthouse while the far-flung network of the branch offices of North American delved into the past of the George Browns of their community in an effort to

128 locate the missing father.

Although he slept in the room with Mrs. Harris and took his meals with her and Mrs. Butterfield, little Henry was actually a good deal more at large in the Schreibers' apartment. He was allowed to browse in the library, and began to read omnivorously. Mrs. Schreiber every so often would take him shopping with her or to an afternoon movie, while it became an invariable Sunday morning ritual that he and Mr. Schreiber would repair to the Sheep Meadow in Central Park with ball, bat, and glove, where little Henry, who had an eye like an eagle and a superb sense of timing, would lash sucker pitches to all corners of the lot for Mr. Schreiber to chase. This was excellent for Mr. Schreiber's health, and very good for his disposition as well. Afterward they might feed the monkeys in the zoo, or roam through the Ramble, or engage a rowboat on the lake and paddle about. Man and boy quickly formed an engaging friendship.

Thus relieved of most of the actual care of the boy, and with more time on her hands since she acted now more in an advisory capacity to the staff she had helped Mrs. Schreiber carefully to select, Mrs. Harris came to the sudden realization that she was no longer pulling her weight in the search for the father of little Henry.

It was all very well for Mr. Schreiber to say that if the man could be found his organization would do the job, but after all the main reason for coming to America was to conduct this search herself, a search she had once somewhat pridefully stated she would bring to a successful conclusion.

She remembered the massive conviction she had felt that if only she could get to America she would solve little Henry's problems. Well, here she was in America, living off the fat of

the land, and slacking while somebody else looked to the job that she herself had been so confident of doing. The least she could do was to investigate the Browns of New York.

"Go to work, Ada 'Arris," she said to herself, and thereafter on her afternoons and evenings off, and in every moment of her spare time, she initiated a systematic run-through of the Geo. and G. Browns listed in the telephone directories of Manhattan, Bronx, Brooklyn, Queens, and Richmond.

Although she might have done so and saved herself a lot of time and energy, Mrs. Harris refused to descend to anything so crude as ringing up the scattered Browns on the telephone and asking them if they had ever served in the U. S. Air Force in Great Britain and married a waitress by the name of Pansy Cott. Instead, she paid them personal visits, sometimes managing to check off two and three in a day.

Familiar with the London tubes, the New York subway systems held no terrors for her, but the buses were something else again, and, used to London civility, she soon found herself embroiled with one of the occupational neurotics at the helm of one of the northbound monsters who, trying to make change, operate his money-gobbling gadget, open and close doors, shout out street numbers, and guide his vehicle through the tightly packed lanes of Yellow Cabs, limousines, and two-toned cars, bawled at her to get to the rear of the bus or get the hell off, he didn't care which.

"Is that 'ow it is?" Mrs. Harris snapped at him. "You know what would happen to you if you spoke to me like that in London? You'd find yerself on your bum sitting in the middle of the King's Road, that's what you would."

132   The bus driver heard a not unfamiliar accent and turned

around to look at Mrs. Harris. "Listen, lady," he said, "I been over there with the Seabees. All them guys over there gotta do is drive the bus."

Injustice worked upon people of her own kind always touched Mrs. Harris's sympathy. She patted the driver on the shoulder and said, "Lor' love yer, it ain't no way to speak to a lydy, but it ain't human either for you to be doing all that —I'd blow up meself if I had to. We wouldn't stand for that in London either—trying to make a bloomin' machine out of a human being."

The driver stopped his bus, turned around, and regarded Mrs. Harris with amazement. "Say," he said, "you really think that? I'm sorry I spoke out of turn, but sometimes I just gotta blow my top. Come along, I'll see that you get a seat." He left the wheel, quite oblivious to the fact that he was tying up traffic for twenty blocks behind him, took Mrs. Harris by the hand, edged her through the crowded bus, and said, "O.K., one of you mugs get up and give this little lady a seat. She's from London. Whaddayou want her to do—get a lousy impression of New York?"

There were three volunteers. Mrs. Harris sat down and made herself comfortable. "Thanks, ducks," she grinned as the driver said, "O.K., Ma?" and went forward to his wheel again. He felt warm inside, like a Boy Scout who had done his good deed for the day. This feeling lasted all of ten blocks.

In a short time Mrs. Harris both saw and learned more about New York and New Yorkers and the environs of its five boroughs than most New Yorkers who had spent a lifetime in that city.

There was a George Brown who lived near Fort George in 133

Upper Manhattan not far from the Hudson, and for the first time Mrs. Harris came upon the magnificent view of that stately river, with the sheer walls of the Jersey Palisades rising opposite, and through another who dwelt near Spuyten Duyvil she learned something of this astonishing, meandering creek which joined the Hudson and East rivers and actually and physically made an island of Manhattan.

A visit to another Brown at the exactly opposite end of Manhattan, Bowling Green, introduced her to the Battery, that incredible plaza overwhelmed by the skyscrapers of the financial district, at the end of which the two mighty arms of water—East and North rivers, as the Hudson is there called—merged into the expanse of the Upper Bay with such seagoing traffic of ocean liners, freighters, tugs, ferryboats, yachts, and whatnot afloat as Mrs. Harris could not have imagined occupied one body of water. Not even through Limehouse Reach and the Wapping Docks back home was water traffic so thick.

For the first time in her life Mrs. Harris felt dwarfed and overpowered. London was a great, gray, sprawling city, larger even than this one, but it did not make one feel so small, so insignificant, and so lost. One could get one's head up, somehow. Far up in the sky, so high that only an airplane could look down upon them, the matchless skyscrapers, each with a flag or a plume of steam or smoke at its peak, filled the eye and the mind to the point of utter bewilderment. What kind of a world was this? Who were these people who had reared these towers? Through the canyons rushed and rumbled the traffic of heavy drays, trucks, and gigantic double lorries with trailers, taxicabs beeped their horns, policemen's whistles shrilled, the shipping moaned and hooted—and in the midst of this stood little Ada Harris of Battersea, alone, not quite undaunted.

In the district surrounding 135th Street and Lenox Avenue, known as Harlem, all the Browns were chocolate colored, but nonetheless sympathetic to Mrs. Harris's quest. Several of them had been to England with the Army or Air Force and welcomed Mrs. Harris as a reminder of a time and place when all men were considered equal under Nazi bombs, and color was no bar to bravery. One of them, out of sheer nostalgia, insisted upon her having a pink gin with him. None of them had married Pansy Cott.

Via several George Browns who lived in the Brighton district Mrs. Harris became acquainted with the eastern boundary of the United States, or rather, at that point, New York—the shore with its long, curving, green combers rolling in to crash upon the beaches of that vast and raucous amusement park— Coney Island.

There the Brown she was tailing that day turned out to be a barker at a girlie sideshow. A tall fellow in a loud silk shirt, straw boater, with piercing eyes that held one transfixed, he stood on a platform outside a booth on which there were rather repulsive olios of ladies with very little clothing on, and shouted down a précis of the attractions within to the passing throngs.

Mrs. Harris's heart sank at the thought that such a one might be the father of little Henry. Yet in the vulgarity of the amusement park she felt not wholly out of place, for with the cries of the barkers, the snapping of rifles in the shooting gallery, the rushing roar of the thrill rides, and the tinny cacophany of the carousel music it reminded her of White City, or any British fun fair, doubled.

Between spiels George Brown, barker, listened to her story with attention and evident sympathy, for when she had finished he said, "It ain't me, but I'd like to find the bastard and punch him one on the nose. If you ask me, he married the girl and took a powder. I know a lot of guys like that."

Mrs. Harris defended little Henry's father vigorously, but the barker remained skeptical. He said, "Take my advice, ma'am, and don't trust none of them GIs. I know them." Mr. Brown had never been in England, but his grandmother had been English and this formed a bond between Mrs. Harris and himself. He said, "Would you like to come back and meet the girls? They're as nice a bunch of kids as you could want. I'll pass you into the show first."

Mrs. Harris spent a pleasant half hour watching Mr. Brown's assortment of "kids" doing bumps, grinds, hulas, and cooch dances, after which she was introduced to them and found, as Brown had said, that they were as described, good-natured, modest about their art, and far cleaner in speech than many of the celebrities who came to the Schreiber parties. She went home after an interesting evening, but no nearer finding the man she sought, though the barker promised to keep an eye out for him.

She learned to like many parts of Brooklyn, where her search took her, for the older and quieter portions of this borough on the other side of the East River, where the brown-stone houses stuck against the side of one another, as like as peas in a pod for block upon block, sometimes shaded by

trees, reminded her somewhat of London far away across the sea.

Since she took the Browns as they came in alphabetical order, one George she found was a ships' chandler who lived over his shop on the waterfront of the Lower East Side. Here again she was an infinitesimal speck in the grand canyons of the downtown skyscrapers, but, standing on the cobbled pave by the docks that smelled of tar and spices, she looked up to the great arches and wondrous spiderweb tracery of the Manhattan and Williamsburg bridges, across which rumbled electric trains and heavy traffic with such a shattering roar that it seemed to be the voices of those vast spans themselves shouting down to her.

On a visit to the Staten Island George Browns via the Staten Island Ferry, Mrs. Harris found one of them to be a tugboat captain working for the Joseph P. O'Ryan Towing Company, in command of the twin diesel-engined tug *Siobhan O'Ryan,* who was just leaving to go on duty as Mrs. Harris arrived.

Captain Brown was a pleasant, brawny man of some forty-odd years, with a pleasant wife half his size, who lived in a cheerful flat in St. George not far from the ferry landing. They had once had something in common, for the *Siobhan O'Ryan* had been one of the tugs which had nursed the SS *Ville de Paris* into her berth the day of Mrs. Harris's arrival, and the sharp-eyed little char had noted the unusual name painted on the pilothouse of the tug, and had remembered it.

Those Browns too were fascinated by the saga of the deserted boy and Mrs. Harris's quest for his father. The upshot was that Captain Brown invited Mrs. Harris to come aboard his tug and he would take her for a water-borne ride around Manhattan Island. This she accepted with alacrity, and thereafter was sailed beneath the spans of the great East River bridges, past the glass-walled buildings of the United Nations to look with awe upon the triple span of the Triborough Bridge, thence over into the Hudson River and down the Jersey side, passing beneath the George Washington Bridge and afforded the view unsurpassed of the cluster of midtown skyscrapers—a mass of masonry so colossal it struck even Mrs. Harris dumb, except for a whisper, "Lor' lumme, yer carn't believe it even when you see it!"

This turned out to be one of the red-letter days of her stay in America, but of course it was not the right Mr. Brown either.

There was a George Brown in Washington Square who painted, another in the garment district of Seventh Avenue who specialized in "Ladies' Stylish Stouts," yet another in Yorkville who operated a delicatessen and urged Mrs. Harris to try his pickles—free—and one who owned a house in the refined precincts of Gracie Square, an old gentleman who reminded her somewhat of the marquis and who, when he had heard her story, invited her in to tea. He was an American gentleman of the old school who had lived in London for many years in his youth and wished Mrs. Harris to tell him what changes had taken place there.

She found Browns who had been airmen in the war, and soldiers, and sailors, and marines, and many of course who had been too young or too old to fill the bill.

Not all were kind and patient with her. Some gave her a brusque New Yorkese brush-off, saying, "Whaddaya trying to hand me about being married to some waitress in England? Get lost, willya? I got a wife and t'ree kids. Get outta here before you get me in trouble."

Not all who had been to London were enamored of that city and, learning that Mrs. Harris came from there, said that if they never saw that dump again it would be too soon.

She interviewed Browns who were plumbers, carpenters, electricians, taxi drivers, lawyers, actors, radio repairmen, laundrymen, stock brokers, rich men, middle-class men, laboring men, for she had added the City Directory to her telephone list. She rang the doorbells in every type and kind of home in every metropolitan neighborhood, introducing herself with, "I hope I ain't disturbin' you. My name's 'Arris —Ada 'Arris—I'm from London. I was looking for a Mr. George Brown who was in the American Air Force over there and married an old friend of mine, a girl by the name of Pansy Cott. You wouldn't be 'im, would you?"

They never were the one she sought, but in most cases she had to tell the story of the desertion of little Henry, which almost invariably fell upon interested and sympathetic ears, due as much to her personality as anything else, so that when she departed she had the feeling of leaving another friend behind her, and people who begged to be kept in touch.

Few native New Yorkers ever penetrated so deeply into their city as did Mrs. Harris, who ranged from the homes of the wealthy on the broad avenues neighboring Central Park, where there was light and air and the indefinable smell of the rich, to the crooked downtown streets and the slums of the Bowery and Lower East Side.

140   She discovered those little city states within the city, sections

devoted to one nationality—in Yorkville, Little Hungary, the Spanish section, and Little Italy down by Mulberry Street. There was even a George Brown who was a Chinese and lived on Pell Street in the heart of New York's Chinatown.

Thus in a month of tireless searching the George Browns of the metropolitan district provided her with a cross section of the American people, and one which confirmed the impression she had of them from the soldiers they had sent over to England during the war. By and large they were kind, friendly, warmhearted, generous, and hospitable. Most of them were so eager to be helpful, and many a George Brown promised to alert all the known others of his clan in other cities in aid of Mrs. Harris's search. So many of them had an appealing, childlike quality of wanting to be loved. She discovered about them a curious paradox: on their streets they were filled with such hurry and bustle that they had no time for anyone, not even to stop for a stranger inquiring the way—they simply hurried on, unseeing, unhearing. Any who did stop turned out to be strangers themselves. But in their homes they were kind, charitable, neighborly, and bountiful, and particularly generous hosts when they learned that Mrs. Harris was a foreigner and British, and it was warming to her to discover that the Americans had never forgotten their admiration for the conduct of the English people during the bombing of London.

But there was yet something further that this involuntary exploration of New York did for Mrs. Harris. Once she lost her awe of the great heights of the buildings to which she was frequently whisked sickeningly by express elevators that leapt thirty floors before the first stop, as well as the dark, roaring canyons they created of the streets, something of the 141 extraordinary power and grandeur, and in particular the youth of this great city, and the myriad opportunities it granted its citizens to flourish and grow wealthy, impressed itself upon her.

This and her glimpses of other cities made her glad that she had brought little Henry to his country. In him, in his independence of spirit, his cleverness, resourcefulness, and determination, she saw the qualities of youth-not-to-be-denied visible on all sides about her in the great city. For herself it was indeed all too much as scene piled upon scene—Midtown, East Side, West Side, New Jersey, Long Island, Westchester—and experience upon experience with these friendly, overwhelming Americans, but it was not a life to which she could ever adapt herself. Little Henry, however, would grow into it, and perhaps even make his contribution to it, if he might only be given his chance.

And this, of course, was the continuing worry, for none of this brought her any closer to the conclusion of her search. None of the George Browns was the right one, or could even so much as give her a clue as to where or how he might be found.

And then one day it happened, but it was not she who succeeded—it was none other than Mr. Schreiber. He came home one evening and summoned her to his study. His wife was already there, and they were both looking most queer and uneasy. Mr. Schreiber cleared his throat several times ostentatiously, and then said, "Sit down, will you, Mrs. Harris?" He cleared his throat again even more portentously. "Well," he said, "I think we've got your man."

Nineteen At this abrupt, and though not wholly unexpected, but still startling piece of news, Mrs. Harris leapt from the edge of the seat she had taken as though propelled by the point of a tack, and cried, "Blimey—'ave you? 'Oo is he? Where is he?"

But Mr. and Mrs. Schreiber did not react to her excitement and enthusiasm. Nor did they smile. Mr. Schreiber said, "You'd better sit down again, Mrs. Harris. It's a kind of a funny story. You'll want to take a grip on yourself."

Something of the mood of her employers now communicated itself to the little charwoman. She peered at them anxiously. She asked, "What's wrong? Is it something awful? Is 'e in jylc?"

Mr. Schreiber played with a paper cutter and looked down at some papers on his desk before him, and as Mrs. Harris followed his gaze she saw that it was U. S. Air Force stationery similar to the kind she had received, plus a photostatic copy of something. Mr. Schreiber then said gently, "I think I'd better tell you, it's—ah—I'm afraid, someone we know. It's Kentucky Claiborne."

Mrs. Harris did not receive the immediate impact of this statement. She merely repeated, "Kentucky Claiborne little 'Enry's dad." And then as the implications of the communication hit her with the force of an Atlas missile she let out a howl. "Ow! What's that you say? 'IM little 'Enry's dad? It can't be true!"

Mr. Schreiber eyed her gravely and said, "I'm sorry. I don't like it any better than you do. He's nothing but an ape. He'll ruin that swell kid."

Waves of horror coursed through Mrs. Harris as she too   143 contemplated the prospect of this child who was just begin-ning to rise out of the mire falling into the hands of such a one. "But are you sure?" she asked.

Mr. Schreiber tapped the papers in front of him and said, "It's all there in his Air Force record—Pansy Cott, little Henry, and everyone."

"But 'ow did you know? 'Oo found out?" cried Mrs. Harris, hoping that somewhere, somehow yet a mistake would have occurred which would nullify this dreadful news.

"I did," said Mr. Schreiber. "I should have been a deteca-tive, I always said so—like Sherlock Holmes. I got a kind of a nose for funny business. It was while he was signing his contract."

Mrs. Schreiber said, "It was really brilliant of Joel." Then her feelings too got the better of her, and she cried, "Oh, poor dear Mrs. Harris, and that poor, sweet child—I'm so sorry."

"But I don't understand," said Mrs. Harris. "What's it got to do with 'is contract?"

"When he signed it," said Mr. Schreiber, "he used his real name, George Brown. Kentucky Claiborne is just his stage name."

But there was a good deal more to it as Mr. Schreiber told the story, and it appeared that he really had displayed acumen and intelligence which would have done credit to a trained investi-gator. It seemed that when all the final details were settled and Kentucky Claiborne, Mr. Hyman, his agent, Mr. Schreiber, and the battalions of lawyers for each side gathered together for the signing of the momentous contract and Mr. Schreiber cast his experienced eye over it, he came upon the name "George

Brown" typed at the bottom and asked, "Who's this George Brown feller?"

Mr. Hyman spoke up and said, "That's Kentucky's real name—the lawyers all say he should sign with his real name in case some trouble comes up later."

Mr. Schreiber said that he felt a queer feeling in his stomach —not that for a moment he suspected that Claiborne could possibly be the missing parent. The qualm, he said, was caused by the contemplation of how awful it would be if by some million-to-one chance it might be the case. They went on with the signing then, and when George Brown alias Kentucky Claiborne thrust his arm out of the sleeve of his greasy black leather jacket to wield the pen that would bring him in ten million dollars, Mr. Schreiber noticed a number, AF28636794, tattooed on his wrist.

Mr. Schreiber had asked, "What's that there number you've got on your wrist, Kentucky?"

The hillbilly singer, smiling somewhat sheepishly, had replied, "That's mah serial number when Ah was in the goddam Air Force. Ah could never remember it nohow, so Ah had it tattooed."

With a quick wit and *sang-froid* that would have done credit to Bulldog Drummond, the Saint, James Bond, or any of the fictional international espionage agents, Mr. Schreiber had committed the serial number to memory, written it down as soon as the ceremony was over and he was alone, and had his secretary send it on to Air Force Headquarters in the Pentagon Building in Washington. Three days later it was all over: back had come the photostat of the dossier from the Air Force records, and Mr. Kentucky Claiborne was unquestionably the 145

George Brown who had married Miss Pansy Amelia Cott at Tunbridge Wells on April 14, 1950, and to whom on September 2 a son was born, christened Henry Semple Brown. To make matters completely binding, a copy of the fingerprints were attached and a photograph of an irritable-looking GI who was incontrovertibly Mr. Kentucky Claiborne ten years younger and minus his sideburns and guitar.

Mrs. Harris inspected the evidence while her mind slowly opened to the nature and depth of the catastrophe that had suddenly overwhelmed them. The only worse thing that could befall little Henry than to be brought up in the poverty-stricken, loveless home of the Gussets was to be reared by this ignorant, selfish, self-centered boor who despised everything foreign, who had hated little Henry on sight, who hated everything and everyone but himself, who cared for nothing but his own career and appetites, and who now would have a vast sum of money to splash about and cater to them.

Mrs. Harris in her romantic fancy had envisioned the unknown, faceless father of little Henry as a man of wealth who would be able to give the child every comfort and advantage; she was shrewd enough to realize that unlimited wealth in the hands of such a person as Claiborne would be deadlier than poison, not only to himself but to the boy. And it was smack into the fire of such a situation and into the hands of such a man that Mrs. Harris was plunging little Henry after snatching him from the frying pan of the horrible Gussets. If only she had not given way to the absurd fancy of taking little Henry to America. With the ocean between, he might still have been saved.

Mrs. Harris left off inspecting the document, went and sat down again because her legs felt so weak. She said, "Oh dear —oh dear!" And then, "Oh Lor', what are we going to do?" Then she asked hoarsely, "'Ave you told 'im yet?"

Mr. Schreiber shook his head and said, "No, I have not. I thought maybe you'd want to think about it a little. It is you who brought the child over here. It's really not up to us. It is you who must decide whether you will tell him."

At least it was a breathing spell. Mrs. Harris said, "Thank you, sir. I'll have to fink," got up off her chair, and left the room.

When she entered the kitchen Mrs. Butterfield looked up and gave a little scream. "Lor' love us, Ada," she yelped. "You're whiter than yer own apron. Something awful 'appened?"

"That's right," said Mrs. Harris.

"They've found little 'Enry's father?"

"Yes," said Mrs. Harris.

"And 'e's dead?"

"No," wailed Mrs. Harris, and then followed it with a string of very naughty words. "That's just it—'e ain't. 'E's alive. It's that [further string of naughty words] Kentucky Claiborne." Into such depths of despair was Mrs. Harris plunged by what seemed to be the utter irretrievability of the situation, the burdens that she had managed to inflict upon those who were kindest to her, and the mess she seemed to have made of things, and in particular the life of little Henry, that she did something she had not done for a long time—she resorted to the talisman of her most cherished possession, her Dior dress. 147

She removed it from the cupboard, laid it out upon the bed, and stood looking down upon it, pulling at her lip and waiting to absorb the message it had to give her.

Once it had seemed unattainable and the most desirable and longed-for thing on earth. It had been attained, for there it was beneath her eyes, almost as crisp and fresh and frothy as when it had been packed into her suitcase in Paris.

Once, too, the garment had involved her in a dilemma which had seemed insoluble, and yet in the end had been solved, for there it was in her possession.

And there, too, was the ugly and defiling scar of the burned-out velvet panel and beading which she had never had repaired, as a reminder of that which she knew but often forgot, namely that the world and all of which it was composed —nature, the elements, humans—were inimical to perfection, and nothing really ever wholly came off. There appeared to be a limitless number of flies to get into people's ointment.

The message of the dress could have been read: Want something hard enough and work for it, and you'll get it, but when you get it it will either prove to be not wholly what you wanted, or something will happen to spoil it.

But even as her eyes rested upon the garment which she had once struggled so valiantly to acquire, she knew in her heart that there were other values, and that they simply did not apply to the trouble in which she now found herself. In the dilemma which had arisen at the last moment and which had threatened collapse to the whole adventure of the Dior dress, she had been helped by someone else. In this dilemma which faced her now, whether to turn a child she had grown to love over to a man who was obviously unfit to be his father, or send him back to the horrors of his foster parents, Mrs. Harris knew that no one could help her—not the Schreibers, certainly not Mrs. Butterfield, or even Mr. Bayswater, or her friend the marquis. She would have to make the decision herself, it would have to be made quickly, and whichever, she knew she would probably never have another moment's quiet peace in her own mind. That's what came of mixing into other people's lives.

For a moment as she looked down upon the mute and inanimate garment it appeared to her almost shoddy in the light of the work and energy it had cost her to acquire it. It was only she who had felt pain when the nasty little London actress to whom she had lent the gown in a fit of generosity one night, had returned it to her, its beauty destroyed by her own negligence and carelessness. The dress had felt nothing. But whichever she did with little Henry Brown, whether she revealed him to this monstrously boorish and selfish man as his son, or surrendered him to the hateful Gussets, little Henry would be feeling it for the rest of his life—and so would Ada Harris. There were many situations that a canny, bred-in-London char could by native wit and experience be expected to cope with, but this was not one of them. She did not know what to do, and her talisman provided no clue for her.

The dress broadcast superficial aphorisms: "Never say die; don't give up the ship; if at first you don't succeed, try, try again; it's a long lane that has no turning; it is always darkest before dawn; the Lord helps those who help themselves." 149

None of them brought any real measure of solace, none of them solved the problem of a life that was still to be lived— that of little Henry.

She even saw clearly now that she had overemphasized— others would have called it overromanticized—the boy's position in the Gusset household. Had he actually been too unhappy? Many a boy had survived kicks and cuffs to become a great man, or at least a good man. Henry had had the toughness and the sweetness of nature to survive. Soon he would have grown too big for Mr. Gusset to larrup any further, he would have had schooling, vocational perhaps, got a job, and lived happily enough in the environment into which he had been born, as had she and the millions of others of her class and situation.

She became overwhelmed suddenly with a sense of her own futility and inadequacy and the enormity of what she had done, and, sitting down upon the bed, she put her hands before her face and wept. She cried not out of frustration or self-pity, but out of love and other-pity. She cried for a small boy who, it seemed, whatever she did, was not to have his chance in the world. The tears seeped through her fingers and fell onto the Dior dress.

Twenty Thereafter, when she had recovered somewhat, she rejoined Mrs. Butterfield, and far, far into that night and long after little Henry had gone to sleep blissfully unconscious of the storm clouds gathering over his head, they debated his

fate.

All through the twistings and turning of arguments, hopes, fears, alternating harebrained plans and down-to-earth common sense, Mrs. Butterfield stuck to one theme which she boomed with a gloomy reiteration, like an African drum: "But, dearie, 'e's 'is father, after all," until Mrs. Harris, almost at her wits' end from the emotional strain brought on by the revelation, cried, "If you say that once more, Vi, I'll blow me top!" Mrs. Butterfield subsided, but Mrs. Harris could see her small mouth silently forming the sentence, "But 'e is, you know."

Mrs. Harris had been involved in many crises in her life, but never one that had so many facets which tugged her in so many different directions, and which imposed such a strain upon the kind of person she was and all her various natures.

Taken as only a minor example of the kind of things that kept cropping up, she had sworn to get even with Kentucky Claiborne for striking little Henry; but now that Mr. Claiborne—or rather, Mr. Brown—was little Henry's father, he could hit him as much as he liked.

From the beginning Mrs. Harris had set herself stonily against doing what she knew she ought to do, which was to turn little Henry over to his blood-and-legal father and wash her hands of the affair. The Schreibers had given her the way out. By not telling Claiborne and leaving the matter up to her they had indicated their sympathy and that they would not talk —only they, she, and Mrs. Butterfield would ever know the truth.

But what then would become of the boy? Bring him back to the Gussets? But how? Mrs. Harris had lived too long in a world of identity cards, ration cards, passports, permits, 151 licenses—a world that in effect said you did not exist unless you had a piece of paper that said you did. Little Henry existed officially in a photostat of the American Air Force records, a London birth certificate, and nowhere else. He had been illegally removed from Britain, and had even more illegally entered the United States. She felt it in her bones that if they tried to get him back the same way they had brought him over they would get caught. She would not have cared for herself, but she could not do it to her already sorely tried friend Violet Butterfield.

Keep little Henry to themselves secretly? Even should they with Mr. Schreiber's help succeed in getting him back to England—not very likely, the unspeakable Gussets were too close for comfort. True, they had not kicked up a fuss over the kidnaping. Obviously there had not been a peep out of them, or Mrs. Harris would have heard via the police. But with little Henry back they would most certainly claim him, for he had his uses as a drudge.

She saw likewise how fatally wrong her fantasy had been about little Henry's parents. It was not Pansy Cott who was to blame, but George Brown—mean, ignorant, vengeful, and intrinsically bad. Pansy had simply used her nut and done the child a good turn when she refused to accompany her husband to America. Unquestionably Brown had just not sent her any money for the support of the child.

Yet a decision would have to be made and she, Ada Harris, must accept the responsibility of making it.

Most deeply painful and overriding every other consideration was the love—feminine, human, all-embracing—that she felt for the boy, and her deep-seated wish to see him happy. She had let her life become inextricably entangled with that of the child, and now there was no escaping it. Like all people who play with fire, she knew that she was in the process of getting herself badly burned.

And through all her arguments, deliberations, and meditations, Mrs. Butterfield boomed her theme: "But, love, after all, 'e *is* the father. You said how 'appy 'e'd be to 'ave 'is little son back, and 'ow 'e'd soon enough take 'im away from the Gussets. 'E's entitled to 'ave 'im, ain't 'e?"

This was the bald, staring, naked, unavoidable truth whichever way one twisted, squirmed, or turned, and the documents in Mr. Schreiber's hands put the seal onto it. George Brown and Henry Brown were united by the ties of blood. So now at four o'clock in the morning Mrs. Harris gave in. She breathed a great sigh and said with a kind of humility that touched the other woman more than anything in their long friendship, "I guess you're right, Vi. You've been more right through all of this all along than I have. 'E's got to go to 'is father. We'll tell Mr. Schreiber in the morning."

And now Mrs. Harris's battered, tired, and sorely tried mind played her a dirty trick, as so often minds will that have been driven to the limit of endurance. It held out a chimera to her, a wholly acceptable solace to one who was badly in need of it. Now that the decision was made, how did they not know that under the softening influence of a little child, George Brown-Kentucky Claiborne would not become another person? Immediately and before she was aware of it, Mrs. Harris was back again in that fantasy land from which practically all of her troubles had sprung.

Everything suddenly resolved itself: Claiborne-Brown had 153 cuffed little Henry when he had thought him an interfering little beggar, but his own son he would take to his bosom. True, he had bellowed his scorn of Limeys—the boy was only half a Limey, the other at least fifty per cent of one hundred per cent American Brown.

All of the old daydreams returned—the grateful father overjoyed at being reunited with his long-lost son, and little Henry brought to a better life than he had ever known before, and certainly this would be true from a financial standpoint; he would never again be hungry, or ragged, or cold; he would be forever out of the clutches of the unspeakable Gussets; he would be educated in this wonderful and glorious country, and would have his chance in life.

As for George Brown, he needed the softening influence of little Henry as much as the boy needed a father. He would succumb to the charm of the boy, give up his drinking, reform his ways in order to set his son a good example, and thus become twice the idol of American youth he already was.

The conviction grew upon Mrs. Harris that she had fulfilled the role of fairy godmother after all. She had done what she had set out to do. She had said, "If I could only get to America I would find little 'Enry's father." Well, she *had* got to America, she *had* found the child's father—or at least had been instrumental in his finding—the father *was* a millionaire as she had always known he would be. "Then dry your tears, Ada 'Arris, and still your worries, and write at the bottom of the page, 'Mission accomplished,' smile, and go to bed."

It was thus the treacherous mind lulled her and let her go to sleep without ever so much as dreaming what awaited her
154   on the morrow.

George-Kentucky Claiborne-Brown was waiting uneasily in Mr. Schreiber's study in the penthouse, whither he had been summoned, the next afternoon after lunch, and this uneasiness increased as Mr. and Mrs. Schreiber entered the room together, followed by Mrs. Harris, Mrs. Butterfield, and an eight- going on nine-year-old boy known as Little Henry.

Mr. Schreiber motioned his own side to sit and said to the performer, "Sit down, Kentucky. We have something rather important to talk to you about."

The too easily aroused ire began to shine in the singer's eyes. He knew what the meeting was all about all right, and he wasn't having any of it. He took up a kind of a defiant stand in a corner of the room and said, "If you-all think you're going to come over me for givin' that kid a poke, you can guess again. The little bastard was annoyin' me at mah rehearsin'. I tol' him to beat it—he got fresh and Ah belted him one. And what's more, Ah'd do it again. Ah tol' you Ah didn't like foreigners any more'n Ah liked niggers. All they have to do is keep out of mah way, and then nobody is goin' to have any trouble."

"Yes, yes," said Mr. Schreiber testily, "we know all that." But now that he had Kentucky safely under contract he was no longer compelled to be as patient or put up with as much. "But that isn't what I've asked you to come here to talk about today. It's something quite different. Sit yourself down and let's get at it."

Relieved somewhat that the purpose of the get-together was not to chew him out for slapping the child, Kentucky sat on a chair back-to-front and watched them all suspiciously out of his small, mean eyes.

Mr. Schreiber said, "Your right name is George Brown, and you did your military service in the U. S. Air Force from 1949 to 1952."

Kentucky set his jaws. "What if Ah am and what if Ah did?"

Mr. Schreiber, who appeared to be enjoying himself—indeed, he now relinquished the role of detecative and was seeing himself as Mr. District Attorney—said, "On the fourteenth of April, 1950, you married a Miss Pansy Amelia Cott in Tunbridge Wells, while you were still in the Air Force, and approximately five months or so later a son was born to you, christened Henry Brown."

"What?" shouted Kentucky. "Man oh man, are you real crazy? You're just nothin' but off. Ah never heard of any of those people."

Mrs. Harris felt as though she were taking part in a television play, and that soon she would be called upon to speak her lines, lines that in anticipation of this scene she had rehearsed to herself and thought rather effective—slightly paraphrased from films and stories she remembered. It was to go something like this: *"Mr. Claiborne, I have a great surprise for you, and one that may cause you some astonishment. In my neighborhood in London there lived a lonely child, starved, beaten and abused by cruel foster parents, unbeknownst to his father in far-off America. I—that is to say, we, Mrs. Butterfield and I—have rescued this child from the clutches of the unfeeling monsters into whose hands he had fallen and brought him here to you. That child is little Henry here, none other than your own natural son. Henry, go over and give your dad a great big hug and kiss."*

156   While Mrs. Harris was going over this speech and clinging

to her fancy to the last, Mr. Schreiber uncovered the papers on his desk and Kentucky, attracted by the rustle, looked over and saw the photostatic copy of his Air Force record, plus the photograph of himself. It cooled him off considerably. "Your serial number in the Air Force was AF28636794, like it's tattooed on your wrist," said Mr. Schreiber, "and your record up to the date of your discharge is all here, including your marriage and the birth of your son."

Kentucky glared at Mr. Schreiber and said, "So what? What if it is? What business is that of anyone? Ah deevo'ced the woman—she was a no-good slut. It was all done legal and proper in accordance with the laws in the state of Alabama, and Ah got the papers that say so. What's all this about?"

Mr. Schreiber's interrogation continued as inexorably as his fancy told him it should. "And the boy?" he asked. "Have you any idea where he is or what has become of him?"

"What's it to you? And why don't you mind your own business?" Kentucky snarled. "Ah signed a contract to sing for your lousy network, but that don't give you no right to be askin' no personal questions. Anyway, Ah deevo'ced the woman legal and proper and contributed to the support of the child. Last I heard of him he was bein' looked after by his mother and gittin' along fine."

Mr. Schreiber put down the papers, looked across his desk, and said, "Tell him, Mrs. Harris."

Thus taken by surprise and thrown an entrance cue entirely different from the one she had expected, Mrs. Harris went completely up in her lines and blurted, "It's a lie! 'E's 'ere —this is 'im right 'ere sitting next to me."

Kentucky's jaw dropped and he stared over at the three, 157

with the child in the middle, and yelled, "What? That little bastard?"

Mrs. Harris was on her feet in a flash, ready for battle, her blue eyes blazing with anger. "'E ain't no little bastard," she retorted. "'E's your flesh and blood, legally married like it sez in those pypers, and I brought 'im to you all the way over 'ere from London."

There was one of those silences during which father looked at son, and son looked at father, and between them passed a glance of implacable dislike. "Who the hell asked you to?" Kentucky snarled.

How it happened Mrs. Harris never would have known, but there she was, Samaritan and Fairy Godmother Extraordinary, suddenly forced upon the defensive. "Nobody asked me," she said. "I did it on me own. The little tyke was bein' beaten and starved by them 'orrid Gussets. We could hear 'im through the walls. I said to Mrs. Butterfield, 'If his dad in America knew about this, 'e wouldn't stand for it, not for a minute'"—Mrs. Butterfield here gave a corroborative nod— "'he'd want 'im out of there in a flash.' So here we are. Now what 'ave you got to say to that?"

Before he could reply something that might have been unprintable, from the twist that his mouth had taken, Mrs. Schreiber, who saw that Mrs. Harris was floundering and things getting out of hand, interpolated quickly, "Mrs. Harris and Mrs. Butterfield live right next door to these people— the Gussets—they were the foster parents—that is to say, Henry's mother boarded the child with them after she remarried, and when the money stopped coming and they couldn't find her they began to abuse the child. Mrs. Harris couldn't bear it and brought him over here to you. She is a good woman and had the best interests of the child at heart and——"

Here she suddenly realized that her explanations were sounding just as lame and flustered as Mrs. Harris's had a moment ago, and she subsided in confusion, looking to her husband for help.

"That's about the way of it, Kentucky," said Mr. Schreiber, stepping into the breach, "though I think maybe it could have been better put. When she brought him over here Mrs. Harris didn't know who the father was, except she figured when she located him and he found out how much the kid needed him and what was happening to him, he'd take over."

Kentucky clucked his tongue and snapped his knuckles in a curious kind of a rhythm he sometimes used in a ballad, and when he had finished he said, "Oh she did, did she?" He then looked over at Mrs. Harris and Mrs. Butterfield and said, "Listen, you two interferin' old bitches, you know what you can do with that brat? You can take him right back where he come from, wherever that was. Ah didn't ask you to bring him over here, Ah don't want him, and Ah ain't goin' to have him. Ah'm just a little ol' country boy, but Ah'm smart enough to know mah public don't want me hooked up with no deevo'ce and no kid, and if you try any funny business about tryin' to make me take him, Ah'll call the pack of you a bunch of dirty liars, tear up mah contract, and then you can go whistlin' for Kentucky Claiborne—and Ah got ten million hundred per cent American kids that'll back me up."

Having delivered himself of this homily, Claiborne let his glance wander around the little group, where it lingered not so much as a second upon his son, and then said, "Well,   159

folks, I guess that'll be about all. Reckon Ah'll be seein' you."
He got up and shambled out of the room.

Mr. Schreiber gave vent to his feelings. "That dirty low-life!" he said.

Mrs. Butterfield threw her apron over her head and ran for the kitchen.

Mrs. Harris stood, ashen-faced, and repeated, "I'm an interferin' old bitch." And then said, "I've done it now, 'aven't I?"

But the loneliest figure was that of little Henry, who stood in the center of the room, the large eyes and the too-large head now filled with more wisdom and sadness than had ever before been collected there, while he said, "Blimey, I wouldn't want 'im for a dad."

Mrs. Schreiber went over, took the child in her arms, and wept over him.

But Mrs. Harris, faced with the last and total collapse of all her dreams and illusions, was far too shattered even to weep.

Twenty-one Mrs. Harris's mind, which previously had tricked her so naughtily into believing that Kentucky Claiborne would receive his child with open arms and from then on exude nothing but sweetness and light, now did her a kindness. It simply blanked out completely. It permitted her to get to her room, take off her clothes, don a nightdress and get into bed, and thereafter drew a merciful curtain over all that had happened. Had it not done so, the fierce pride of Mrs. Harris would not have been able to have borne the humiliation she had undergone and the collapse of the beautiful dreams of a good life for a little boy that she had nourished for so long, and to which she had given so much of herself. She lay with her eyes wide open, staring up at the ceiling, seeing, hearing, and saying nothing.

It was Mrs. Butterfield's shrill scream of fear and anguish upon making the discovery that gave the alarm and brought Mrs. Schreiber rushing into the kitchen.

"Oh, ma'am," said Mrs. Butterfield after she had been calmed somewhat, "it's Ada. Something's wrong with 'er— something 'orrible. She just lies there kind of like she's 'arf dead and won't say a word."

Mrs. Schreiber took one look at the small, wispy figure tucked away in the bed, looking even smaller and wispier now that all the air of her ebullient ego had been let out of her, made one or two attempts to rouse her, and, when they failed, rushed to her husband and telephoned to Dr. Jonas, the family physician.

The doctor came and did those professional things he deemed necessary, and then came out to the Schreibers. "This woman has had a severe shock of some kind," he said. "Do you know anything about her?"

"You're telling me," said Mr. Schreiber, and then launched into the story of what had happened, culminating with the scene with the unwilling father.

The doctor nodded and said, "Yes, I can see. Well, we shall have to wait. Sometimes this is Nature's way of compensating for the unbearable. She seems to have a good deal of vitality, and in my opinon it will not be too long before she begins to come out of it."

But it was a week before the fog which had descended upon Mrs. Harris began to lift, and the impetus for its dispelling arose in a somewhat extraordinary manner.

The Schreibers were hardly able to endure waiting, because of what had taken place in the interim and the new state of affairs which they were dying to impart to Mrs. Harris, certain that if once she returned to herself it would contribute to her rapid convalescence.

It began with a telephone call for Mrs. Harris shortly before lunch one day, and which Mrs. Schreiber answered. Mr. Schreiber was likewise present, as his office was not far from his home and he liked to return for lunch. What seemed to be a most elegant and cultured English voice said, "I beg your pardon, but might I have a word with Mrs. Harris?"

Mrs. Schreiber said, "Oh dear, I am afraid not. You see, she's ill. Who is this, please?"

The voice echoed her, "Oh dear," and added, "Ill, you say? This is Bayswater speaking—John Bayswater of Bayswater, London. Nothing serious, I trust."

Mrs. Schreiber in an aside to her husband said, "It's someone for Mrs. Harris by the name of Bayswater," then into the phone, "Are you a friend of hers?"

Mr. Bayswater replied, "I believe I may count myself such. She requested me to telephone her on my next visit to New York, and certainly my employer, the Marquis de Chassagne, the French ambassador, will be anxious about her. I am his chauffeur."

Mrs. Schreiber remembered now, and with her hand over the mouthpiece quickly transferred the information to her husband.

"Leave him come up," said Mr. Schreiber. "What harm can it do? And maybe it could do her some good—you never know."

Twenty minutes later an anxious Mr. Bayswater, elegant in his gray whipcord uniform, his smart chauffeur's cap in one hand, appeared at the door of the Schreiber apartment and was ushered by them into Mrs. Harris's bedroom, with the worried and, since Mrs. Harris's illness, perpetually snuffling Mrs. Butterfield looming in the background.

Mrs. Harris had been taking mild nourishment, tea and bread and butter or light biscuits, but otherwise had given no sign of recognition of anyone about her.

Mr. Bayswater, it seemed, had been a very worried man over a period, and it was this worry which had brought him to New York. The most perfect Rolls to which he had ever been wedded had developed a mysterious noise in its innards, a noise barely audible to any but the trained ear of Mr. Bayswater, to whom it sounded like the crackling of midsummer thunder, and whom it was driving up the wall. It was unbearable to him that this should happen in a Rolls, and even more so in one he had had the honor to select and test himself.

All his skill, knowledge, acumen, and experience of years had not enabled him to locate the seat of this disturbance, and thereafter for him there had been no rest or solace, and he had brought the car to New York for a more thorough stripping down and examination at the Rolls service station there. He had delivered the machine to the garage and thought that in a chat with Mrs. Harris he might relieve his mind of the burdens imposed upon it by this imperfection.

But now that he stood looking down upon this pale ghost of a woman, the apple cheeks shrunken and the heretofore naughty, snapping, and merry little eyes clouded over, all thoughts of the stricken Rolls were swept from his head and for the first time in many, many years he was conscious of a new kind of heartache. He went over to her bedside, sat down, took one of her hands in his, quite oblivious to the watching Schreibers and Mrs. Butterfield, and, lapsing as he was inclined to when under a great emotional strain, said, " 'Ere, 'ere, Ada, this will never do. What's all this about?"

Something in his voice penetrated. Perhaps it was the two dropped aitches which turned the key in the lock and opened the door for Mrs. Harris. She turned her head and looked directly into the grayish, elegant, and austere face of Mr. Bayswater, noted the curly gray hair, almost patrician nose and thin lips, and said in a weak voice, " 'Ullo, John. What brings you up 'ere?"

"Business," replied Mr. Bayswater. "You told me to get on the blower if I came this way. I did, and they told me you weren't too perky. What's it all about?"

They all thrust to the fore now, Mrs. Butterfield yammering, "Ow, Ada, thank the Good Lord you're better," Mrs. Schreiber crying, "Oh, Mrs. Harris, how wonderful! You're better, aren't you? We've been so worried," and Mr. Schreiber shouting, "Mrs. Harris! Mrs. Harris, listen! Everything's all right— we've got the most wonderful news for you!"

164   The face and the voice of Mr. Bayswater had indeed put

Mrs. Harris's cart back on the road by recalling the most delectable drive up from Washington with him, and an even more delectable stop at a famous roadside restaurant on the way, where she had had a most extraordinarily tasty soup of clams, leeks, potatoes, and cream, called New England clam chowder. It would have been better for her had she been able to live within these memories a little longer, but alas, the cries of the others soon broke the spell and brought her back to the realization of the catastrophe she had precipitated. She covered her face with her hands and cried, "No, no! Go away —I can't fyce anyone. I'm a silly, interferin' old woman who spoils everything she lays her 'ands on. Please go away."

But Mr. Schreiber was not to be denied now. He pushed forward, saying, "But you don't understand, Mrs. Harris— something terrific has happened since you've been——I mean since you haven't been well. Something absolutely stupendous! We're adopting little Henry! He's ours. He's going to stay with us, if you don't mind. You know we love the kid, and he loves us. He'll have a good home with us and grow up into a fine man."

Mrs. Harris was yet very ill in her soul and thus only half heard what Mr. Schreiber was saying, but since it seemed to have something to do with little Henry, and he sounded cheerful and happy about it, she took her hands from her face and gazed about her, looking greatly like an unhappy little monkey.

"It was Henrietta's idea," Mr. Schreiber explained, "and right away the next day I got ahold of Kentucky and had another talk with him. He ain't a bad guy when you get to know him more. It's just he don't like kids. He's got a thing about he'd lose his following if it came out he'd been married and divorced abroad and had a kid who was half English. So I said if he wouldn't have any objections we'd like to adopt the kid, Henrietta and I, and bring him up like our own son."

" 'You're an interferin' old bitch. Take the brat back to England,' 'e sez to me," quoted Mrs. Harris. " 'Is own father."

"But you don't understand," Mr. Schreiber said. "He isn't making any trouble. It all works out one hundred per cent for everybody. The kid's an American citizen, so he's got a right to be here. Kentucky's his legal father, and the evidence is right there in the Air Force files. We've written to England to get a birth certificate for the little fellow. There'll be no trouble with anybody because, as his father, Claiborne's got the right to have him here with him. The legal beagles are making out the adoption papers, and he's going to sign 'em as soon as they're ready."

Some penetration had been achieved now, for Mrs. Harris turned a slightly more cheerful countenance to Mr. Schreiber and said, "Are you sure? 'E'd 'ave a good 'ome with you."

"Of course I'm sure," cried Mr. Schreiber, delighted that he had registered. "I'm telling you, the guy was tickled to death to get rid——I mean, he's glad too that the kid's going to be with us."

Mrs. Schreiber thought that Mrs. Harris had gone through enough for that particular period, nudged her husband, and said, "We can talk more about it later, Joel—maybe Mrs. Harris would like to be alone with her friend for a bit now." Mr. Schreiber, film magnate, detecative and District Attorney, showed himself to be an exemplary husband as well by getting it in one and saying, "Sure, sure. We'll run along now."

When they had gone, Mrs. Butterfield too having tactfully withdrawn, Mr. Bayswater said, "Well, there you are. It's turned out all right, hasn't it?"

A remnant of the black wave of disillusionment that had engulfed her swept over Mrs. Harris again, for it had been such a beautiful dream, and she had steeped herself in it for so long. "I'm a fool," she said. "An interferin' busybody who ain't got the brynes to mind 'er own business. I've done nothing but cause everybody trouble. Me, who was so cock-sure about turnin' up little 'Enry's father in America. Lor', what a bloody mess I've made of things."

Mr. Bayswater went to give her a little pat on her hand, and was surprised to find he was still holding it clutched in his, so he gave it a squeeze instead, and said, "Go on with you. You shouldn't talk like that. It looks to me as though you managed to turn up not one but two fathers for little 'Enry. Two for the price of one isn't so bad."

The merest whisper of a smile softened Mrs. Harris's face for the first time, but she was not going to let go her megrims and guilt feelings quite so easily. "It could've turned out 'orrible," she said, "if it 'adn't been for Mr. Schreiber. What would've become of the little fellow if it 'adn't been for 'im?"

"What would have become of the little fellow if it hadn't been for *you?*" said Mr. Bayswater, and smiled down at her.

Mrs. Harris smiled back and said, "What brings you up to New York, John?"

Now his own troubles came sweeping back over Mr. Bays-water, and his elegant frame in the whipcord uniform gave a slight shudder, and he passed the back of his hand over his brow. "It's the Rolls," he said. "She's developed a noise in her and I can't find it. I'm like to go out of me mind—that is to say, go out of my mind. I've been at it for over a week now and can't find it. It isn't in the gearbox, and it isn't in the silencer of the oil-bath air cleaner. I've had the rear axle down, and it isn't there. I've looked through the hydraulic system, and taken down the engine. It isn't in the distributor head, and there's nothing the matter with the water pump. Sometimes you get a click in the fan belt, but it isn't that."

"What's it like?" Mrs. Harris asked, thus showing herself to be a woman who could be interested in a man's world as well.

"Well, it isn't exactly a knocking or a scraping—nor even a ticking or a pipping," explained Mr. Bayswater, "but it's there. I can 'ear it. You shouldn't hear anything in a Rolls-Royce—not *my* Rolls-Royce. It's under the seat somewhere, but not exactly—rather more in back, and it's driving me up the wall. It's somehow as if the Good Lord had said, 'You there, so proud and stuck-up about your automobile—perfect you said it was. I'll show you perfect. Let's see you get around *this*, Mr. Stuck-up.' It ain't that I'm stuck-up," explained Mr. Bayswater, "it's just that I love Rolls cars. All me life I've never loved anything else. All me life I've been looking for the perfect one, and this was it—until now."

The distress on the handsome features of the elderly chauffeur touched Mrs. Harris's heart, and made her forget her own troubles, and she wished genuinely to be able to comfort him as he somehow had managed to comfort her. Some long-ago memory was nibbling at her newly awakened and refreshed mind, and it suddenly gave her a sharp nip. "I 'ad a lady once I did for some years ago," she said, "a proper Mrs. Rich-Bitch she was. She 'ad a Rolls and a chauffeur, and one day I heard   169 'er say, 'James, there's something rattling in the back of the car. Find it before I 'as a nervous breakdown.' Coo, 'e nearly went orf 'is loaf tryin' to locate it. 'Ad the car took apart and put together twice, and then come across it by accident. You know what it was?"

"No," said Mr. Bayswater. "What was it?"

"One of 'er 'airpins that fell out and slipped down be'ind the seat. But that couldn't be it, could it? The marquis don't wear 'airpins."

Mr. Bayswater had a lapse, a real, fat, juicy lapse. "Blimey," he cried. "Gaw' bleedin' blimey!" And on his face was the look of the condemned who hears that he has been reprieved by the governor. "I think you've got it! The marquis doesn't wear hairpins, but last week I drove Madame Mogahdjibh, the wife of the Syrian ambassador, home after a party. She was loaded with them—big black ones. Ada, my girl, here's the smacker you didn't get on the boat," and he leaned down and kissed her brow, then leapt to his feet and said, "I'm going to find out, I'll be seeing you," and rushed from the room.

Left to herself, Mrs. Harris reflected upon this matter of perfection for which humans seem to strive, as exemplified by Mr. Bayswater's distress over something that had come to shatter the perfection of the finest car in the world, and she thought that perhaps perfection belonged only to that Being on High Who sometimes seemed friendly to humans, and sometimes less so, and at other times even a little jealous.

Had she been asking too much? "Yes," something inside Mrs. Harris answered vehemently, "far too much." It had not been only fairy godmother she had been trying to play, it had been almost God, and the punishment that had followed had

170

been swift and sure. And then her thoughts turned back to her Dior dress which had been so exquisite and so perfect, and the ugly burnt-out panel that was in it to remind her that though the dress itself had been spoiled, out of the experience had come something even better in the shape of some wonderful friendships.

And thence it was but a step to the comfort that if she had been less than successful in her avowed mission of reuniting little Henry with his father, it had not been wholly a failure. Nothing in life ever was a complete and one hundred per cent success, but often one could well afford to settle for less, and this would seem to be the greatest lesson one could learn in life. Little Henry was out of the hands of the unspeakable Gussets, he had acquired adoptive parents who loved him and would help him to grow into a good and fine man; she herself had experienced and learned to feel an affection for a new land and a new people. Thus to grouse and grumble and carry on in the face of such bounty now suddenly took on the color of darkest ingratitude. The Schreibers so happy, little Henry equally so—how dare she not be happy herself because her ridiculous and vainglorious little dream had been exploded.

"Ada 'Arris," she said to herself, "you ought to be ashymed of yerself, lyin' about 'ere on yer back when there's work to be done." She called out loud, "Violet."

Mrs. Butterfield came galumphing into the room like an overjoyed hippopotamus. "Did you call me, dearie? Lor' bless us, but if you ain't lookin' like yer old self again."

"''Ow about making me a cuppa tea, love?" said Mrs. Harris. "I'm gettin' up."

171

Twenty-two The early summer enchantment of May and June in New York, with girls out in their light summer dresses, the parks in full bloom and the skies clear and sunny, had given way to the sweltering, uncomfortable humidity and heat waves of July. The Schreiber household was running like clockwork, with a permanent staff now trained and disciplined by Mrs. Harris, the final formalities by which the Schreibers became the adopted parents and permanent guardians of Henry Brown completed, and the child installed in his own quarters in the Schreiber house. The passage of time was bringing nearer two events about which something would have to be done.

One of them was the arrival of vacation time, the annual exodus from the hot city to the more temperate climes of mountains or seashore, and the other was the approaching expiration on the seventeenth of July of the visitors' visas to the United States of the dames Butterfield and Harris.

Mr. and Mrs. Schreiber held several conferences together on the subject, and then one evening Mrs. Butterfield and Mrs. Harris were called into Mr. Schreiber's study, where they found the couple seated, looking portentous.

"Dear Mrs. Harris and dear Mrs. Butterfield, don't stand, do sit down, please," said Mrs. Schreiber. "My husband and I have something to discuss with you."

The two Englishwomen exchanged glances and then gingerly occupied the edges of two chairs, and Mrs. Schreiber said, "Mr. Schreiber and I have taken a small cottage in Maine by the sea for little Henry and ourselves, where we intend to spend several months and rest quietly. Mr. Schreiber is very tired after the work of reorganizing his company, and we don't wish to do any entertaining. We can leave our flat here in the hands of our staff, but we were wondering whether you and Mrs. Butterfield wouldn't accompany us to Forest Harbor and look after little Henry and myself while we are there. Nothing would make us happier."

The two women exchanged looks again, and Mr. Schreiber said, "You don't have to worry about your visitors' visas—I got friends in Washington who can get you a six months' extension. I was going to do that anyway."

"And afterward in the fall when we come back . . . well, we rather hoped you'd stay with us too," Mrs. Schreiber continued. And then in a rush blurted, "We hoped somehow we might persuade you to stay with us for always. You see, little Henry loves you both, and—so do we—I mean, we feel we owe you a debt of gratitude we can never repay. If it hadn't been for you we never should have had little Henry for our very own, and he already means more to us than my husband and I are able to say. We just don't ever want you to go. You won't have to work hard, and you can always make your home with us. Will you stay? Will you come with us this summer?"

In the silence that ensued after this plea the two Londoners exchanged looks for the third time, and Mrs. Butterfield's chins began to quiver, but Mrs. Harris as spokesman and captain of the crew remained more in control, though she too was visibly touched by the offer. "Lor' bless you both for your kindness," she said. "Violet and I have been discussing nothing else for days. We're ever so sorry—we carn't."

Mr. Schreiber looked genuinely nonplussed. "Discussing it for days?" he said. "Why, we've only sprung it on you now. We haven't known about it ourselves until just recent——" 173

"We've seen it coming," said Mrs. Harris, and Mrs. Butterfield, all her chins throbbing now, put a corner of her apron to one eye and said, "Such dear, kind people."

"You mean you knew all about the house we've taken in the country and that we'd want you and Mrs. Butterfield to come with us there?" Mrs. Schreiber asked in astonishment.

Mrs. Harris was not at all abashed. She replied, "One 'ears things about the 'ouse. Little pitchers have big ears, and rolling stones have bigger ones. What is there to talk about in servants 'all except what goes on in the front of the 'ouse?"

"Then you won't stay?" said Mrs. Schreiber, a note of unhappiness in her voice.

"Love," said Mrs. Harris, "there's nuffink we wouldn't want to do for you to repay you for your kindness to us, and for giving little 'Enry a 'ome and chance in life, but we've talked it over—we carn't, we just carn't."

Mr. Schreiber, who saw his wife's disappointment, said, "What's the matter? Don't you like America?"

"Lor' love yer," said Mrs. Harris fervently, "it ain't that. It's wonderful. There's nuffink like it anywhere else in the world. Ain't that so, Violet?"

Mrs. Butterfield's emotions were such that she was able to do no more than nod acquiescence.

"Well then, what is it?" persisted Mr. Schreiber. "If it's more money you want, we could——"

"Money!" exclaimed Mrs. Harris, aghast. "We've had too much already. We wouldn't take another penny off you. It's just—just that we're 'omesick."

"Homesick," Mr. Schreiber echoed, "with all you've got over here? Why, we've got everything."

"That's just it," said Mrs. Harris. "We've got too much of everything 'ere—we're homesick for less. Our time is up. We want to go back to London." And suddenly, as though it came forth from the deep and hidden wells of her heart, she cried with a kind of anguish that touched Mrs. Schreiber and penetrated even to her husband, "Don't ask us to stay, please—or ask us why."

For how could she explain, even to the Schreibers, who knew and had lived in and loved London themselves, their longing for the quieter, softer tempo of that great, gray, sprawling city where they had been born and reared?

The tall, glittering skyscrapers of New York raised one's eyes into the heavens, the incredible crash and bustle and thunder of the never-still traffic, and the teeming canyons at the bottom of the mountainous buildings excited and stimulated the nerves and caused the blood to pump faster, the glorious shops and theaters, the wonders of the supermarkets, were sources of never-ending excitement to Mrs. Harris. How, then, explain their yearning to be back where gray, drab buildings stretched for seemingly never-ending blocks, or turned to quaint, quiet, tree-lined squares, or streets where every house was painted a different color?

How make their friends understand that excitement too-long sustained loses its pitch, that they yearned for the quiet and the comforting ugliness of Willis Gardens, where the hoofs of the old horse pulling the flower vendor's dray in the spring sounded cloppety-cloppety-cloppety in the quiet, and the passage of a taxicab was almost an event?

What was there to compare, Mrs. Harris and Mrs. Butterfield had decided, in all this rush, scurry, litter and hurry, this neon-lit, electricity-blazing city where they had indeed been thrilled to have been a part of it for a short time, with the quiet comfort of cups of tea that they drank together on alternate evenings in their little basement flats in their own particular little corner of London?

Nor could they, without hurting the feelings of these good people, tell them that they were desperately missing quite a different kind of excitement, and that was the daily thrill of their part-time work.

In London each day brought them something different, some new adventure, some new tidbit of gossip, something good happened, something bad, some cause for mutual rejoicing or mutual indignation. They served not one but each a dozen or more clients of varying moods and temperaments. Each of these clients had a life, hopes, ambitions, worries, troubles, failures, and triumphs, and these Mrs. Harris and Mrs. Butterfield shared for an hour or two a day. Thus instead of one, each of them lived a dozen vicarious lives, lives rich and full, as their part-time mistresses and masters confided in them, as was the custom in London between employer and daily woman.

What would Major Wallace's new girl be like, the one he had carefully explained as his cousin just arrived from Rhodesia, but whom Mrs. Harris knew he had encountered at the Antelope two nights before? What new demands of service to be joyously, fiercely, and indignantly resisted would the Countess Wyszcinska present on the morrow? Did the *Express* have a juicy scandal story of how Lord Whosis had been caught by his wife canoodling with Pamela Whatsis amongst the potted palms at that gay Mayfair party? Mrs. Fford Foulks, she of the twin Fs and the social position of a witty and attractive divorcée, would have been there, and the next afternoon when Mrs. Harris arrived to "do" for her between the hours of three and five she would have the story of what really happened, and some of the riper details that the *Express* had been compelled by the laws of libel to forego.

Then there was the excitement connected with her other bachelor client, Mr. Alexander Hero, whose business it was to poke his nose into haunted houses, who maintained a mysterious laboratory at the back of his house in Eaton Mews, and whom she looked after and mothered, in spite of the fact that she was somewhat afraid of him. But there was a gruesome thrill in being connected with someone who was an associate of ghosts, and she reveled in it.

Even such minor items as whether Mr. Pilkerton would have located his missing toupee, the progress of convalescence of the Wadhams' orange-colored toy poodle, a dear little dog who was always ill, and whether Lady Dant's new dress would be ready in time for the Hunt Ball made each day an interesting one for them.

And furthermore there was the excitement of the sudden decision to discard a client who had gone sour on them or overstepped some rule of deportment laid down by the chars' union, and the great adventure of selecting a new one to take his or her place; the call at the employment office or Universal Aunts, the interrogating of the would-be client, the final decision, and then the thrill of the first visit to the new flat, a veritable treasure palace of new things to be snooped at and gone over.

What was there in New York, even though it was the greatest city in the world, to compare with that?

The littlest things were dragging Mrs. Harris and Mrs. Butterfield homeward. Never had food been presented more enticingly yet, alas, more impersonally, than in the giant supermarket where they shopped. Every chop, every lettuce leaf, every gleaming, scrubbed carrot had its cellophane envelope on its shining counter, washed, wrapped, packed, ticketed, priced, displayed, untouched by human hands. What both Mrs. Butterfield and Mrs. Harris longed for was the homeliness of Warbles's, the corner grocer's shop with its display of tired greens, dispirited cabbages, and overblown sprouts, but smelling of spices and things well remembered, and presided over by fat Mr. Warbles himself. They wanted to see Mr. Hagger, the butcher, slice off a chop, fling it onto the scales with a "There you are, dear, as fine a bit of English lamb as ever you'll set your teeth in. One and tuppence-ha'penny, please," wrap it in a piece of last month's newspaper, and hand it over the counter with the air of one bestowing a great gift.

They had sampled all of the fabulous means of snacking in New York—the palatial Childs with their griddle cakes and maple syrup, to which Mrs. Harris became passionately addicted, the Automats where robots miraculously produced cups of coffee, and even the long drugstore counters where white-coated attendants squirted soda water into chocolate syrup, and produced triple- and quadruple-tiered sandwiches of regal splendor. But the two women born within the sound of Bow Bells, and whom London fitted like a well-worn garment, found themselves yearning for the clatter of a Lyons' Corner House, or the warm redolency and pungent aroma of a fish-and-chips shop.

The bars and grills on Lexington and Third avenues they sometimes visited for a nip were glittering palaces of mirror glass, mahogany, and gilt, each with a free television show included, but the Mesdames Harris and Butterfield longed for the drab mustiness of the Crown close to their demesne, and the comfort of its public bar, where two ladies could sit quietly sipping beer or gin, indulging in refined conversation or an occasional game of darts.

The police of New York were strong, handsome, men, mostly Irish, but they just weren't bobbies. Mrs. Harris remembered with ever-increasing nostalgia the pauses for chats about local affairs with P. C. Hooter, who was both guardian and neighborhood psychiatrist of their street.

The sounds, the smells and rhythms, the skies, the sunsets and the rains of London were all different from those of the fabulous city of New York, and she craved all of them. She yearned even to be lost and gasping in a good old London, green pea-soup fog.

But how convey all this to the Schreibers?

Perhaps the Schreibers with their own memories of a beloved and happy stay in London were more sensitive than she had thought, for they heeded her cry and questioned her no more. Mr. Schreiber only sighed and said, "Well, I suppose when you gotta go, you gotta go. I'll fix it up for you."

Twenty-three Even though it takes place almost weekly in New York, there is always something exciting and dramatic about the sailing of a great liner, and in particular the departure of that hugest of all ships ever to sail the seven seas, the *Queen Elizabeth.*

Especially in the summertime, when Americans swarm to the Continent for their holidays, is the hubbub and hurly-burly at its peak, with the approaches to Pier 90 beneath the elevated highway at Fiftieth Street packed solid with Yellow Cabs and stately limousines delivering passengers and their luggage. The pier is a turmoil of travelers and porters, and aboard the colossal steamer there appears to be one huge party going on, cut into smaller ones only by the walls of the companionways and cabins, as in each room departing passengers entertain their friends with champagne, whisky, and canapés.

There is a particular, infectious gaiety about these farewell parties aboard ship, a true manifestation of a holiday spirit, and of all those taking place on the *Queen Elizabeth* on her scheduled summer sailing of July 16, none was gayer, happier, or more infectious than that which took place in Cabin No. A11, the largest and best apartment in tourist class, where at three o'clock in the afternoon prior to the five o'clock sailing, Mesdames Harris and Butterfield held court from amidst a welter of orchids and roses.

Reporters do not visit tourist class on sailing day, reserving their attentions for the celebrities certain to be spotted in the luxury quarters. In this case they missed a bet, and just as well, for the guests collected at Mrs. Harris's sailing party were not only celebrated but heterogeneous. There was, for instance, the French ambassador to the United States, the Marquis Hypolite 181 de Chassagne, accompanied by his chauffeur, Mr. John Bayswater of Bayswater, London.

Then they would have come upon Mr. Joel Schreiber, president of North American Pictures and Television Company Inc., recently celebrated for his signing of Kentucky Claiborne to a ten-million-dollar contract, accompanied by his wife, Henrietta, and their newly adopted son, Henry Brown Schreiber, aged almost nine.

A fortunate thing indeed that the sharp-eyed minions of the New York press did not see this family, else they would have had some questions to ask of how the erstwhile son of Lord Dartington of Stowe and grandson of the Marquis de Chassagne, whose arrival in the United States had been signalized with story and photograph, had suddenly metamorphosed into the adopted son of Mr. and Mrs. Schreiber.

Further amongst the guests were a Mr. Gregson, a Miss Fitt, and a Mrs. Hodge, respectively butler, parlormaid, and cook of the household staff of the Schreibers.

And finally the party was completed by a number of the George Browns of New York who had fallen for Mrs. Harris, and whom during the course of her search she had added to her ever-growing collection of international friends. There was Mr. George Brown, the barker, very spruce in an alpaca suit, with a gay band on his straw boater; Captain George Brown, master of the *Siobhan O'Ryan,* his muscles bulging through his blue Sunday suit, towing his little wife behind him somewhat in the manner of a dinghy; there was the elegant Mr. George Brown of Gracie Square; two Browns from the Bronx; the nostalgic chocolate-colored one from Harlem; one from Long Island, and a family of them from Brooklyn.

182

The true identity of little Henry's father had been kept a secret, but Mrs. Harris had appraised them all of the happy ending to the affair, and they had come to celebrate this conclusion and see her off.

If the centers of attraction, Mrs. Harris and Mrs. Butterfield, had worn all of the sprays of purple orchids sent them by their guests, they would have staggered under the load. As it was, Mrs. Harris's sense of protocol decreed that they should wear the offering of the Marquis de Chassagne, whose orchids were white and bound with ribbons which mingled the colors of France, Great Britain, and the United States. Waiters kept the champagne flowing and the canapés moving.

Drink, and in particular the bubbly wine, is a necessity at these affairs, for the conversation just before departure tends to stultify, when people rather incline to repeat the same things over and over again.

Mr. Schreiber repeated to the marquis, "The kid's going to be a great ball player. I'm telling you. He's got an eye like Babe Ruth had. I threw him my sinker the other day, figuring he'd be lucky to get a piece of it. You know what he did?"

"No," said the marquis.

"He takes a cut like DiMag used to and hoists the apple into the next lot. What do you think of that?"

"Astonishing," said the marquis, who had not understood a word that Mr. Schreiber had said, beyond meaning that Henry had performed another prodigy of some kind, and remembering that the President of the United States himself seemed to be impressed with the young man's athletic abilities.

"Give my regards to Leicester Square," said Mr. George 183

Brown of Harlem. "Someday I'm going back there. It was good to us boys in the war."

"If I ever run across the George Brown that took a powder on the kid, I'll poke him one just for luck," promised the Coney Island Brown.

"You soi'nly desoive a lotta credit," repeated the Brooklyn Browns.

"Someday we're gonna come over there and look you up," prophesied a Brown from the Bronx.

"I suppose White's and Buck's are just the same," sighed the Gracie Square Brown. "They'll never change."

"Dear," said Mrs. Schreiber for the fourth time, "when you go past our flat on Eaton Square, throw in a kiss for me. I wonder who's living there now." And then wistfully, as she thought of the good days that had been when life was not so complicated, "Maybe you'll even go there and work for them. I'll never forget you or what you did for us. Don't forget to write and tell me how everything is."

Bayswater hovered on the outskirts rather silently and seemingly lost, for what with little Henry, who somehow no longer looked so little, his body having begun to grow to his head size, and all the sadness having been wiped forever out of his eyes, hugging the two women, and the others all making a fuss over them, it seemed impossible to get close to give Mrs. Harris what he had for her.

Yet somehow he contrived to catch her eye and hold it for a moment while he raised his own eyebrows and moved one shoulder imperceptibly in the direction of the door, but sufficient for Mrs. Harris to get the message and escape momentarily from the cordon.

184

" 'Old the fort a minute," she said to Mrs. Butterfield, "while I look what's become of me trunk."

"You won't be gettin' off the boat will yer?" said Mrs. Butterfield in alarm—but Mrs. Harris was already out the door.

Down the passageway a bit, to the accompaniment of the clink of glasses, shrieks of laughter, and cries of farewell from parties in nearby cabins, Mrs. Harris said, "Whew. I didn't know how I was goin' to get away to arsk you—was it a 'airpin?"

In reply Mr. Bayswater reached into the pocket of his uniform where a bulge somewhat interfered with its elegant line, and handed Mrs. Harris a small package. It contained a bottle of Eau de Cologne, and represented a major effort on the part of the chauffeur, for it was the first such purchase and the first such gift he had ever made to a woman in his life before. Affixed to the outside of it with a rubber band was a large and formidable-looking black wire hairpin.

Mrs. Harris studied the specimen. "Lumme," she said, "ain't it a whopper?"

Mr. Bayswater nodded. "There she is. Something like that gets into a Rolls and it can sound like your rear end's dropping out. I'd never have looked for it if it hadn't been for you. The scent's for you."

Mrs. Harris said, "Thank you, John. And I'll keep the 'airpin as a souvenir. I suppose we'd better go back."

But Mr. Bayswater was not yet finished, and now he fussed and stirred uneasily with a hand in his pocket, and finally said, "Ah—Ada, there was something else I wanted to give you, if you wouldn't mind." He then withdrew his hand from his pocket and disclosed therein something that Mrs. Harris had

185

no difficulty in recognizing with even an odd little thrill of forewarning as to what it might be about.

"They're the keys of my flat," said Mr. Bayswater. "I was wondering if sometime you might have a moment to look in for me, just to make sure everything's all right—64 Willmott Terrace, Bayswater Road, Bayswater."

Mrs. Harris looked down at the keys in Mr. Bayswater's palm and felt a curious warmth surging through her such as she had not known since she was a young girl.

Mr. Bayswater too was feeling very odd, and perspiring slightly under his linen collar. Neither of them was aware of the symbolism of the handing over of the keys, but both felt as though they were in the grip of something strange, momentous, and pleasant.

Mrs. Harris took them out of his hand, and they felt hot to the touch, as he had been clutching them. "Coo," she said, "by now I'll bet the plyce could do with a bit of a turnout. Do you mind if I dust about a bit?"

"Oh, I didn't mean *that*," said Mr. Bayswater. "I wouldn't dream of asking you. It was just that I felt that if you might look in occasionally—well then—I'd know everything was all right."

"You'll be a long time away, won't you?" said Mrs. Harris.

"Not so long," said Mr. Bayswater. "I'll be home in another six months. I've given my notice."

Mrs. Harris looked horrified. "Given your notice, John! Why, whatever's got into you? What will the marquis do?"

"He understands," said Bayswater somewhat mysteriously. "A friend of mine is taking over."

"But the car," said Mrs. Harris. "Ought you to be leaving it?"

"Oh, I don't know," said Mr. Bayswater. "Maybe one ought to take things a little easier. The affair of the hairpin came as a bit of a shock to me. Opened my eyes somewhat. It's time I was thinking of retiring, anyway. I've saved up all the money I shall ever need. I'd only signed to come out for a year. If I stay away longer I find I get a bit homesick for Bayswater."

"Like me," said Mrs. Harris, "and Willis Gardens. Cozy, that's what it is, at night with the curtains drawn and Mrs. Butterfield in for a cuppa tea." And then instinctively but unconsciously paraphrasing, "There's no plyce like it."

"Will I be seeing you when I get back?" asked Mr. Bayswater, the question showing his state of mind, since he had just turned over the keys to his flat.

"If you 'appen to come by," said Mrs. Harris with equal and elaborate falseness, since she now held his keys in her own gnarled hand. "Number five's the number, Willis Gardens, Battersea. I'm always in after seven, except Thursdays when Mrs. Butterfield and I go to the flicks. But if you'd like to drop me a post card we could make it another night."

"No fear," said Mr. Bayswater. "I will. Well, I suppose we'd better be getting back to the rest."

"Yes, I guess we 'ad."

They went. In Mrs. Harris's hand was the earnest and the promise that someday in the not too far distant future she would see him again. And in the emptiness of Mr. Bayswater's pocket where the keys no longer were, was the guarantee that with them in her possession he would see Ada Harris again. 187

As they came back into the cabin Mr. Schreiber was just finishing putting little Henry through his catechism for the benefit of the marquis. For the first time it seemed to her that Mrs. Harris saw the difference in the child, the sturdiness that had come to his figure, and the fact that all the wariness and expectation of cuffs and blows had left his expression. Little Henry had never been a coward or a sniveler—his had been the air of one expecting the worst, and usually getting it. So soon, and already he was a whole boy; not too much longer and he would be on his way to becoming a whole man. Mrs. Harris was not versed in official prayers of gratitude, and her concept of the Deity was somewhat muddled and ever-changing, but He loomed up to her as benign now, as kind and loving as ever she could conceive of someone. And to her concept of that figure which looked rather like the gentle, bearded figure of the Lord depicted on religious post cards, she said an inward "Thank you."

"What are you going to be when you grow up?" asked Mr. Schreiber.

"A baseball player," replied little Henry.

"What position?" asked Mr. Schreiber.

Little Henry had to reflect over that one for a moment, and then said, "Middle fielder."

"Center fielder," corrected Mr. Schreiber. "That's right. All the great hitters played in the outfield—Ruth, Cobb, DiMaggio, Meusel. What team you going to play on?"

Little Henry knew that one all right. "The New York Yankees," he said.

"See?" said Mr. Schreiber, glowing. "A regular American already."

The hooter hooted three times, there was a trampling of feet on the companionway without, and an attendant passed by banging on a gong and shouting, "Visitors ashore, please. All ashore that's going ashore." Now as they moved to the door with Mrs. Butterfield sobbing audibly, the farewells were redoubled: "Good-by, Mrs. Harris. God bless you," cried Mrs. Schreiber. "Don't forget to look who's living in our apartment."

"Good-by, madame," said the marquis, who bent over her, took her hand in his, and brushed it with his white mustache. "You should be a very happy woman for the happiness you have brought to others—including, I might add, to me. All in all, it was a real lark. I have told everyone my grandson has returned to his father in England, so there will be no further difficulties."

"Good-by—good luck!" echoed all the Browns.

"Good-by—good luck!" said Mr. Schreiber. "You need anything, you write and tell me. Don't forget, we got a branch office over there. They can fix you up anytime."

Little Henry went up to them with a new shyness, for in spite of everything, his experiences and his inexperience, he was still a small boy, and emotions, particularly those strongly felt, embarrassed him. He could not see into his future, but there was no doubt in his mind as to the present, as well as the past from which these two women had rescued him, even though the memory of his life with the Gussets was already beginning to fade.

But Mrs. Butterfield had no such inhibitions. She gathered little Henry to her, drowning his face in her billowy bosom and interfering seriously with his breathing as she hugged, cuddled, wept, and sobbed over him, until finally Mrs. Harris had to say to her, "Come on, dearie. Don't carry on so. 'E isn't a baby any more—'e's a man now," and thus earning more gratitude from the boy even than for his rescue.

He went to Mrs. Harris and, throwing his arms about her neck, whispered, "Good-by, Auntie Ada. I love you."

And those were the last words spoken as they filed out, and until they all stood at the end of the pier and watched the magnificent liner back out into the busy North River, brass portholes reflecting the hot July sun, and the thousand faces dotting the gleaming white of the decks and superstructure. Somewhere forward would be the dots that represented Mrs. Butterfield and Mrs. Harris. The great siren of the liner bayed three times in farewell, and the Marquis Hypolite de Chassagne pronounced a kind of a valedictory.

"If I had my way," he said, "I would rear a statue in a public square to women like that, for they are the true heroines of life. They do their duty day in, day out, they struggle against poverty, loneliness, and want, to preserve themselves and raise their families, but still they are able to laugh, to smile, to find time to indulge in dreams." The marquis paused, reflected a moment, sighed, and said, "And this is why I would rear them their statue, for the courage of these dreams of beauty and romance that still persist. And see," he said, "the wondrous result of such dreaming."

The *Queen Elizabeth* bayed again. She was now broadside to the pier, and in midstream. Her screws threshed and she began to glide down toward the sea. The marquis raised his hat.

Aboard the liner Mrs. Harris and Mrs. Butterfield, the eyes of both reddened with tears now, repaired to their cabin, whence came their steward.

191

"Twigg's the name," he said. "I'm your steward. Your stewardess is Evans. She'll be along in a minute." He gazed at the banked-up flowers. "Cor' blimey, if it don't look as if somebody died in 'ere."

"Coo," said Mrs. Harris, "you watch yer lip or you'll find out 'oo died in 'ere. Them flowers is from the French ambassador, I'll 'ave you know."

" 'Ello, 'ello," said the steward as the familiar accent fell upon his ears, and not at all abashed by the reproof, "Don't tell me now, but let me guess—Battersea, I'll wager. I'm from by Clapham Common meself. You never know 'oo yer meets travelin' these days. I'll 'ave yer tickets, please."

And then as he departed, "Cheer-oh, lydies. You can rely on Bill Twigg and Jessie Evans to look after yer. Yer couldn't be on a better ship."

Mrs. Harris sat on her bed and sighed with contentment. "Clapham Common" had fallen gently and gratefully upon her ears too. "Lor' love yer, Violet," she said. "Ain't it good to be 'ome?"